THE LEGACY SERIES

SERIES TITLES

Close to a Flame
Colleen Alles

American Animism
Jamey Gallagher

Keeping What's Best Left Kept Secret
David Ricchiute

Soaked
Toby LeBlanc

The Path of Totality
Marie Zhuikov

Shocker in Gloomtown
Dan Libman

The Continental Divide
Bob Johnson

The Three Devils and Other Stories
William Luvaas

The Correct Response
Manfred Gabriel

Welcome Back to the World: A Novella & Stories
Rob Davidson

Greyhound Cowboy and Other Stories
Ken Post

Close Call
Kim Suhr

The Waterman
Gary Schanbacher

Signs of the Imminent Apocalypse and Other Stories
Heidi Bell

What We Might Become
Sara Reish Desmond

The Silver State Stories
Michael Darcher

An Instinct for Movement
Michael Mattes

The Machine We Trust
Tim Conrad

Gridlock
Brett Biebel

Salt Folk
Ryan Habermeyer

The Commission of Inquiry
Patrick Nevins

Maximum Speed
Kevin Clouther

Reach Her in This Light
Jane Curtis

The Spirit in My Shoes
John Michael Cummings

The Effects of Urban Renewal on Mid-Century America and Other Crime Stories
Jeff Esterholm

What Makes You Think You're Supposed to Feel Better
Jody Hobbs Hesler

Fugitive Daydreams
Leah McCormack

Hoist House: A Novella & Stories
Jenny Robertson

Finding the Bones: Stories & A Novella
Nikki Kallio

Self-Defense
Corey Mertes

Where Are Your People From?
James B. De Monte

Sometimes Creek
Steve Fox

The Plagues
Joe Baumann

The Clayfields
Elise Gregory

Kind of Blue
Christopher Chambers

Evangelina Everyday
Dawn Burns

Township
Jamie Lyn Smith

Responsible Adults
Patricia Ann McNair

Great Escapes from Detroit
Joseph O'Malley

Nothing to Lose
Kim Suhr

The Appointed Hour
Susanne Davis

"As subtle as they are piercing, these stories will tear you open and then stitch you back up. The prose is clear-eyed and graceful, never precious or distracting from the narrative and thematic threads that will mean so much to so many: motherhood, deep and abiding friendship, love in all its messy vicissitudes. This collection moved me in ways I didn't know I wanted to be moved."

—NATHAN GOWER
author of *The Act of Disappearing*

"Alles has crafted a moving testament to love, longing, and what we are forced to leave behind if we are to grow. With prose that is both wise and wistful, *Close to a Flame* delivers its readers into the lives of some of the strongest women I've read in recent fiction. Across these stories, Alles does what only the keenest writers can: she shows her readers their fullest selves."

—RS DEEREN
author of *Enough to Lose*

"Love burns steadily, appealingly, in *Close to a Flame*, Colleen Alles's brilliant new collection, in which she explores love's various intensities, from high school infatuation, through familial love, to soulmate maturity. But as life-long friends Jaimie and Miriam remind us as we follow them through several of the stories, while getting close to a flame may provide us with an awareness of the dangers involved in getting too close, it will not stop us from suffering minor injuries. Fortunately for us, Alles tends to love's all-too-familiar wounds with compassion and understanding."

—PHILLIP STERLING
author of *In Which Brief Stories Are Told*

CLOSE TO A FLAME

STORIES

COLLEEN ALLES

CORNERSTONE PRESS
UNIVERSITY OF WISCONSIN-STEVENS POINT

Cornerstone Press, Stevens Point, Wisconsin 54481
Copyright © 2025 Colleen Alles
www.uwsp.edu/cornerstone

Printed in the United States of America by
Point Print and Design Studio, Stevens Point, Wisconsin

Library of Congress Control Number: 2025932048
ISBN: 978-1-960329-65-3

Cornerstone Press titles are produced in courses and internships offered by the
Department of English at the University of Wisconsin–Stevens Point.

DIRECTOR & PUBLISHER
Dr. Ross K. Tangedal

EXECUTIVE EDITORS
Jeff Snowbarger, Freesia McKee

EDITORIAL DIRECTOR
Brett Hill

SENIOR EDITOR
Ellie Atkinson

PRESS STAFF
Paige Biever, Mai Kao Hang, Karlie Harpold, Christiana Niedwiecki, Eva Nielson,
Sophie McPherson, Madison Schultz, Ava Willett

for my family

&

to be honest, this one's for Jessie, too

ALSO BY COLLEEN ALLES:

FICTION

The Hound of Thornfield High
Master of Arts
Skinny Vanilla Crisis

POETRY

Bonfires & Other Vigils
After the 8-Ball

STORIES

Restoring Notre-Dame   1

Fifth Circle   9

The Only Private Place   19

Antique Desk   38

Visitor's Pass   47

Arrangements   57

Psychic Reading   69

Loggerhead   79

Cusping   88

Baby Registry   102

Stag's   111

Interwoven   121

Bachelorette Party   130

Whisper Moment   137

In Tandem   147

Christ at Heart's Door   151

Acknowledgements   159

Stories hold your life together.
—Greg Pape

RESTORING NOTRE-DAME

Miriam and Jamie

Miriam anchors herself to my body, wobbling as she removes her foot from her shoe, the high heel of which has jammed itself between two crumbly bricks. At just a hair over five feet tall, Miriam looks more like my little sister than my best friend. We've been taken for sisters. Sometimes, at the bar, Miriam tells boys we are.

"All set?" I ask.

Miriam nods. I feel glad then we've turned away from the Irish bar. A walk and a break will do us good.

"Let's go to The Tavern," Miriam says. She's walking more carefully now, minding her heels, and she has both hands on my right elbow.

"I thought you didn't like that place."

"I *hate* The Tavern," she says, "but tonight is about *you*." This bar crawl was her idea. She leans in and kisses me on the cheek, her breath warm on my skin. She bursts out laughing.

"We have to drink until you forget about *what's-his-name*."

Which is Davis. Not David, not Dave. Davis. We began dating last fall. I met him at a party near campus. I had a bad head cold that night, so I wasn't drinking, just sipping. He'd eyed me for a bit, finally approaching when I went to the kitchen for water.

"I'm Davis," he said. He'd hoisted himself onto the counter, poured vodka into a red solo cup, and talked to me until I had to take Miriam home. He was funny. And very cute. He didn't blink when he listened to me talk. He looked down when he smiled.

As I was leaving the party, Davis had handed me his red cup, half-filled with alcohol.

"Oh, no thanks," I had told him. "I'm driving this little lady home."

"No," he said, laughing. "Write down your number." He searched for something to write with and settled on the Sharpie on a far counter.

I'd written my number below his name on the cup. His handwriting was so bad, it looked like his name was *Paris*, not *Davis*.

It wasn't possible then to know that a few weeks later, a fire in Paris would destroy large parts of the Notre-Dame Cathedral—a place I'd put at the top of my list of places I wanted to go someday. When I donated money online that April to the effort to rebuild the cathedral, Miriam teased me. My twenty bucks would buy half a brick, she joked.

Yet I was so tired of watching the news and doing nothing, and I wanted to believe I could do something to help. I wanted to believe something small could matter a lot. I wanted to believe the building could be just as beautiful as it was before all that damage.

IT WAS CASUAL IN THE BEGINNING—the thing with Davis. I let him make the first move and I played it cool until Christmas. By then, I liked him too much to hide it. By February, he was distant. It was too much for him, I guess. *I* was too much.

"Screw that guy," Miriam had said. I'd been with her in the library, trying to study for midterms. We both had two papers to write and little motivation to write them.

It was early March then. Davis had planned a trip to Florida with his brother and two friends for spring break. I had been clingy to suggest he and I do something, he said, although I was having poor luck getting out of my shifts at work anyway. Twenty hours a week, I sat at a desk in a dorm room supervising a floor of freshmen. The north wing of the residence hall was for males, the south for females. Most of my job seemed to be subjecting the respective genders to this important geographical division after curfew.

"We'll do something *fun*," Miriam said, tapping my textbook to get my attention. "Bars. The mall. Let's find some parties. We'll get into trouble. And you'll forget about Davis."

That was a week ago, and while Davis had sent me a text last Sunday to let me know he was home, I'd ignored it.

It hadn't been easy.

"Delete, delete, delete," Miriam had said. "Don't you *dare* respond."

And I hadn't.

I didn't delete it, though. I stared at it on my phone.

Yo, I'm back from Florida. Hope you enjoyed spring break.

"Who says *yo* anyway?" Miriam teased.

"I don't understand if we broke up," I'd said.

She'd shrugged. "Who cares?"

I'd let her question fade into silence, although to me, the answer was obvious.

Me. I cared. A lot.

Davis Fletcher, I thought. *What was so wrong with me?*

THERE'S NO LINE AT THE TAVERN, which is no surprise. It isn't a great bar, but Miriam squeals anyway when we find a table. She goes to the bar to order with a bartender who sports a champion frown. Meanwhile, I take a deep breath, sitting back against my chair.

Miriam is perennially optimistic that we only ever need to buy one round for ourselves; subsequent rounds would come via the generosity of boys. She wasn't wrong.

"There's a *very* cute boy at the bar," Miriam says as she returns to our table. The orange slice perched on the lip of each pint glass gives away that it's Oberon.

"I bet he looks back here in a second," she says, wagging her eyebrows.

"Oh *God*," I say, when he finally does.

"What?" Miriam asks.

"That's Ian Fletcher."

"Ohh," Miriam says, letting the note rise and fall with her voice. "*Shit.*"

From our table, I take a long drink to give my hands and mouth something to do while I watch Ian. He seems to be debating whether it's more awkward to come over and say hi, or to sit at the bar and pretend we hadn't locked eyes.

On New Year's Eve, we'd been at the same party. That was the night Davis sloshed champagne on my blouse, twice, and kissed me at midnight.

"*Uh oh*," Miriam says. "He's coming over."

Ian is a version of Davis. A blurred iteration. He is younger, but taller, and a little thicker around the middle. Arguably more attractive, with long hair he runs his fingers through as he approaches our table. They are a little more than one year apart. Same college. Many shared friends.

Next to me, I feel Miriam wiggle in her chair.

"Hi, Jamie," he says. "Nice to see you again."

"You too," I say. I force my eyes to stay on his and not scan the bar. It's possible Davis is here, but I can't sense him. My heart beats a little faster anyway.

"How was spring break?" Miriam asks.

Ian takes a drink. "It was good. Drove down to Florida. Met up with some friends."

"Oh," Miriam says, drawing out the syllable. "Some *friends*."

If Ian has caught her sarcasm, he doesn't let on.

If Davis is here with Ian, he's either in a different part of the bar, or perhaps outside smoking, in which case, we'd somehow missed him, and in which case he'll be walking through the door at any moment.

Ian seems sincere, though, as he holds my gaze and asks how my break was.

"It was nice," I say, nodding. "I had to work a lot, you know, but it was nice to have a break from studying."

"Did you do anything fun?"

"Hung out with friends," I say vaguely. I remind myself to smile. "Read a few good books, caught up on my binging."

"That's cool," Ian says. "What books—"

"Are you here alone?" Miriam interrupts. Her voice slurs enough to remind me I hold my alcohol better than she does.

"Um," Ian says. He looks to the bar, which gives Miriam and me permission to follow his gaze. "Just friends."

"No *brothers*?" Miriam asks, leaning her head toward Ian.

He smiles but doesn't look uncomfortable. Then he does the one thing that I was probably least expecting: he pulls out the chair he's been touching, far enough to sit down in it. He folds his long legs under the table. He scoots forward, and he leans in toward me.

"Here's the thing about my brother," Ian says. "I love the guy. Obviously."

"Go on," Miriam says.

"He's an idiot," Ian says. He's looking right at me again.

I think about the text message from Davis, the one I've left burning on my phone—the one I've managed to ignore for nearly eight days, and the ability to resist typing anything back to him suddenly feels like one of my life's greatest achievements.

"You're right, he *is* an idiot," Miriam interjects. "Who does he think he is? You guys have been back from Florida for a *week*?"

Ian nods, sticking out his lower lip. I try to remember if Ian kissed a girl on New Year's Eve. I remember one standing by him at that party—a pretty girl in a shimmery silver dress. She'd been hanging on Ian the way I'd been trying not to hang on Davis.

"Yeah, give or take," he says.

"*Give or take?*" Miriam mimics.

Ian frowns, takes another pull from his beer. I wonder if he's hoping he'll hit the bottom of his bottle so he'll have a good reason to excuse himself from our table.

This isn't his problem, and he knows it. Although at the moment, with Miriam on the verge of yelling at Ian, I think this may be my only chance to confirm with Ian the things I have sensed about his older brother for months: that Davis was always a little too far away, that he never liked to feel pinned down—not even by someone who tried very hard to hold him at a good distance.

Ian starts to say something, then stops.

"*What?*" Miriam says. "Just *say* it."

"Miriam," I say.

"No," she says, "this man owes you some answers."

"No," I say again, gently. "He doesn't." I look at Ian. "You don't," I say softly.

"His brother does," she says pointedly. She's slurring a little.

I nod. "Yes. Probably."

I look back at Ian, whose eyes have been moving between the two of us like he's watching a tennis match. He looks, I think, at least a little amused.

I give Ian my best smile. "You don't owe me anything. I think I've got it figured out anyway."

Ian takes another drink from his bottle, sits back in his chair.

"My brother's an idiot," Ian repeats, holding my eyes and smiling.

"Yeah, that's right, he *is* an idiot," Miriam says. Fresh fire is in her words. "You deliver a message to that brother of yours," she says. "You tell him that he's blind not to realize what a treasure this girl is."

Miriam is now holding my hand. "She is the most—she is beautiful, and she is smart—and she is like, kind—and like, *way* better than your brother—"

"I know," Ian says.

I stare at my pint glass. It's almost empty.

"You deliver that message, you hear?" Miriam says.

"I will," Ian says, and his choice to stand up at that point seems involuntary.

I look up to give him an apologetic smile, knowing that as soon as we finish these beers, we are not going to hang around to see if any boys will buy us another round. It's time to take Miriam home, listen to her curse in the streets, see if her heels stick in the spaces between the bricks again.

"You deliver that message," Miriam repeats as Ian stands and pushes his chair in. Before he walks away, he takes his beer and taps it briefly on my pint glass.

"Cheers," he says, winking my way. "I'll see you around."

I would run into Ian around campus about a dozen more times before I graduated. Davis never came back to school that fall, I heard. I did think about the Fletcher brothers years later, the summer I finally made it to Paris, and I saw Notre-Dame, almost fully restored, and admired all the work that had gone into rebuilding such a beautiful, ancient structure.

"WHAT A WANKER," Miriam says as we leave The Tavern ten minutes later. She's somehow adopted a British persona in the time she left me to use the restroom.

Ian is still sitting at the bar as we leave, but he doesn't turn around to look at us again.

"Not Ian," I say.

"No, not Ian. His brother. Ian is a breath of fresh air after a long drought in the desert."

I laugh and put my arm around her. "You're drunk."

"You were supposed to forget his name," Miriam moans. "Not run into his baby brother. I've completely failed you. Let's find another bar." She's leaning her body weight into me as we walk. I listen to the *click-clack* of her shoes on the old bricks like it's a clunky lullaby. It's probably time to call it a night, but now I know that isn't what we're going to do at all.

"Sure," I say. "Where're we going next?"

FIFTH CIRCLE

"It looks like Hogwarts," Jonah had told her once. They were walking up the stone steps to the arched doorway of the high school. She pushed the memory out of her mind for two reasons.

For one, he was right: the high school looked almost magical. It *did* look like something from *Harry Potter.*

The second reason she pushed the memory aside? It made her *love* Jonah, and fiercely, for how smart and how funny he was. And she didn't want to love him right then. She wanted to exude the authority of a parent unhappy with her teenager. Which she was.

In silence, Beth and Jonah passed through the formidable door and walked down the long hallway to the Administration Center. Her heart was pounding hard as she muscled open the door to the principal's office. She knew without looking that she and Jonah were exactly five minutes late for their meeting with Mr. Zeeger. He opened the door, offered a curt smile, and instructed the two of them to sit on the pair of padded chairs across from his desk.

Already, Beth wanted to leave.

Keith had offered—more than once—to come to the meeting with her. For the third or fourth time, however, Beth had let her husband know that morning that she could handle it.

"It'll be fine," she had told him.

"But he's such a *dick*," Keith had said.

Beth had laughed. "I know that," she had said. "And *you* know that. But Jonah doesn't. And we're not going to go into that with him. He doesn't need to know." "I know," Keith had said, stroking his chin. "Still."

"I know," Beth had said, mirroring her husband. "It doesn't get much weirder than this."

"Seriously," Keith had said. "This is like, fifth circle of hell kind of shit."

"I know," Beth had said, sighing, an ocean of things she wanted to say crashing around in her mind like waves.

"FIRST OFF, THANKS FOR COMING," Mr. Zeeger said as he walked to his chair.

Beth felt the corners of her mouth tighten to a pucker, which was sort of like a smile. She looked over at Jonah for the first time since they had gotten out of the Jeep.

Beth had once read an article about how if you want to have a productive conversation with someone, you should have it while in a car. Both people are facing the same direction and are looking at the same thing. Supposedly, that fostered an opportunity for good communication.

The car ride with Jonah, however, had been quiet.

Beth looked over at Jonah, sitting next to her in Mr. Zeeger's office. He had chosen his dark wash jeans with a rip at the knee, she noticed, and had pulled his old gray hoodie over a white t-shirt. The hoodie probably needed to be washed, but it was his favorite, and therefore difficult to get away from him on laundry day. He was also wearing an old baseball cap of Keith's—one that Roger, their puppy, had taken chewing liberties to last year.

And his face.

Somehow, it was possible to assign each of Jonah's features to either herself, or to Keith. Keith's thick eyebrows.

Her slightly crooked nose. Keith's ears. Her almond-shaped eyes. Jonah was, at fifteen, an unapologetically perfect blend of the two of them, and Beth wondered if all mothers felt the way she did when she looked at Jonah.

Probably.

"It's no trouble," Beth answered. She felt proud of her voice: it sounded strong. So far so good. "Thank you for making the time to speak with us," she offered.

There. The hardest part was breaking the ice, she thought. *And that's over now.*

Still, her heart was pounding. She wondered if Jonah was nervous about being in the principal's office. This was a first for him. The three words Beth typically reached for to describe her son were: quiet, nerdy, and smart—not a troublemaker. A kid that teachers praised at conferences.

Jonah was studying the carpet. She wished she could do the same, instead of meeting Mr. Zeeger's gaze. She didn't want Jonah to know she was nervous.

But it wasn't like *she* was the one in trouble. She had never been in trouble as a high school student—at least not with the principal, at least not that she could remember.

But now—

Fifth circle of hell kind of shit.

"I think it's important that we have a conversation about rules," Mr. Zeeger said. "I know Jonah is just a freshman this year…"

BETH REALIZED SHE HAD TUNED him out and snapped back to listening. Was Jonah listening?

Why hadn't she let Keith come with her? She would have had his hand to hold. Of course, Keith couldn't stand to be around Mr. Zeeger, either.

He looked so *different* from the man she used to know. He was a totally different person.

The first time they had kissed, it had been shyly, and after a movie.

They had been sitting on a stone bench outside her college dorm, which was ridiculous in January. They had watched a few passersby in heavy coats, and Beth had said something inane about the reflection of the moon on the snow—knowing she had wanted to kiss him, and he had wanted to kiss her.

It had been sweet, then. *He* had been sweet.

It was hard to remember that Mr. Zeeger had once been a twenty-year-old with shaggy brown hair and—no kidding—one of those tweed jackets with the elbow patches. He wore that jacket to the math class they shared. Trying to get through that class had bored them both.

Their first conversation had been about their instructor's terrible English pronunciation.

"I can't understand a word he's saying," he had whispered, turning around in his chair to talk to Beth. "Can you?"

And then a few weeks later, they were kissing on that bench, and Beth liked him, she really liked him. The kind boy who wore that tweed jacket and smiled so easily. The nice young man who had kissed her and who had wanted to become a history teacher.

Now, sitting across from him, she wondered if he ever thought about those memories, the ones from a lifetime ago.

Was it good to think about those early memories because they were perfect—the stuff of love stories? Or was it better to bury them deep down, letting the weight of the years that followed push and crowd them down to the deep parts of her mind? A reminder that life changes, and that people change, too.

She really wished she had Keith's hand to hold.

Instead, she reached out and took Jonah's hand, and by some great miracle of the heavens, her sometimes moody, quiet, nerdy son, allowed it.

"SO, WHERE DID YOU and Bill *go* during these 'breaks?'" Mr. Zeeger asked, putting air quotes around the word "breaks."

"Just to GameStop," he answered. "The video game store."

"The video game store," Mr. Zeeger repeated, his tone clearly indicating disapproval.

To look at him now, Beth thought.

His shaggy hair was mostly gone. He wasn't bald, but his hair had thinned considerably.

Most men his age couldn't seem to avoid the small belly bulge just above the belt, and Mr. Zeeger was no different. His skin looked worn. He was wearing khakis and brown shoes. He had a tie on. When Beth looked for them, she could see small sweat stains at his armpits.

He also wore a wedding ring. Beth knew he had gotten married shortly after their own engagement had ended. He married a woman they had known loosely through college friends. She was nice enough.

Beth wondered if his wife had been the one to pick out his outfit. She pictured his wife washing his underwear and hanging his clothes up to dry on a line. It was so weird.

From history teacher to high school principal. That was weird, too.

When they were younger, he had never talked about wanting to be a principal. Now, he seemed far more concerned with exercising his power, his authority.

But, Beth thought. *People change.*

She had moved into his small apartment the year he student-taught sophomores. He had come home nearly every day with essays to grade, excited about his students' progress. Their ideas. Their funny stories. Their crushes on one another.

Three weeks before the wedding, though, Beth was boxing up books and throwing her clothes into garbage bags, sobbing loudly enough for Mr. Zeeger—Tony—to hear her from the living room.

But aren't breakups often messy? What a mess theirs had been.

Things between them had been bad for months, and while Beth had read that planning a wedding brought couples together, planning *their* wedding had driven a wedge between them. Tony had grown mean, manipulative. He had grown distant, too. It was as though as soon as they were engaged, he acted like he could treat her however he wanted, which was usually poorly. He ignored her. He gave her one-word answers.

He began to expect that she would do things around their apartment, too. At first, Beth hadn't minded. She would put on the cute "MRS" apron she had received at a bridal shower and clean the house, make dinner, handle the bills, grab the mail.

As the weeks wore on, she grew tired of taking care of all the laundry, all the work at home. He only seemed to notice when she *hadn't* gotten around to something—not when she had gone out of her way to take care of the chores. He didn't seem to realize how hard she was straining to make sure everything looked nice.

Then, she had started to realize that that was what *their* relationship had become in only half a year: something that only looked nice. It wasn't an equal partnership. Tony was showing her what marriage with him would be like.

When people show you who they are, she had once read, believe them. So, she did.

What mistakes had *she* made, though? Beth tried to remember.

She admitted to herself that she had pulled back, too, spending more time with her friends and with her work. She hadn't cheated on Tony, but she had started to find the company of other men at happy hour or at lunch a pleasant reprieve from her home life.

She had stopped working on their wedding plans. It was going to be a small wedding with just their immediate family and some close friends. She had waited for Tony to notice she wasn't asking questions about flowers or itineraries or drink selections. He never did.

Soon, they had stopped spending time together, talking mostly through notes around their apartment. Then, she didn't talk about Tony unless someone else brought him up. She forgot to wear her engagement ring one day after the gym, and then she continued to forget for a month.

The drama of it came back to her in flashes, then, in Tony's—Mr. Zeeger's—office. She hadn't hated anyone before she hated him and had been unprepared for the intensity of the feeling. At twenty-three, it had run as white-hot emotion to her bones.

Why had she hated him so much? Was it how he had changed from someone who dreamed of teaching high school students to a distant, mean man who made her feel trapped, unloved, and lonely?

Did she hate him so much because he had taken the best years of her life—college and just after? Did she hate him because—

Suddenly, while he was in the middle of a sentence, Beth remembered why.

"WE ONLY SKIPPED CLASS because we already know it," Jonah was saying.

"You already know algebra," Mr. Zeeger asked, though not as a question. He looked bemused.

"Yeah," Jonah said. "I had it in eighth grade."

Beth wanted to jump in, but Mr. Zeeger kept lecturing. "So your solution to this issue of already knowing the material, was to skip class every day for two weeks? You and Bill?"

Jonah nodded, a little sheepish.

"Did it ever occur to you to talk to Ms. Grable? Tell her you already knew the material?"

Jonah's cheeks began to redden. "No," Jonah said. "We were bored."

"Pardon?"

"We were bored," Jonah said louder.

"I think what you need to learn," Mr. Zeeger said, leaning back in his chair, "is that there are more *appropriate* ways to deal with your emotions than just leaving. If you feel there is more you would like to be getting out of the class, then you should communicate a little better. If you feel something is missing, for example, instead of simply not showing up for a few weeks in a row, you need to sit down with Ms. Grable and talk to her about—"

Before she knew what was happening, Beth felt herself stand up.

Mr. Zeeger stopped mid-sentence. "Are you all right Mrs. . . . ?" Mr. Zeeger asked, looking down at the papers on his desk.

Before he could say anything else, Beth looked at Jonah who was staring at her, puzzled. "It's just—well, we need to leave," she said suddenly.

"*Excuse* me?"

"Yeah, we're—yeah. That's it. Thank you. Thank you for your time. Come on Jonah," Beth said.

And just like that, Beth walked out of Tony's office, smiling to herself as she heard Jonah following behind.

"THAT WAS *AWESOME*, MOM!" Jonah said as they got into the Jeep. Neither of them had said anything while they walked through the Hogwarts doors. But once in the car, sitting side by side, it was time to talk.

"But I don't get it," Jonah said.

Beth studied him then, again—his beautiful eyes, and the intelligence behind them. She remembered those first harrowing weeks when she and Keith had taken him home from the hospital. How exhausted she was, but how precious Jonah was at three in the morning. How cute he was when he smiled at her in the middle of the night.

And in between her flashbacks of Jonah, she let this memory bubble up one more time before she resolved to let it go forever:

During her break-up with Tony, she had stayed at a friend's place while looking for a new apartment. Painfully, she had had to make several trips back to Tony's to pick up her stuff.

In the movies, breakups are seamless, and usually set to music. Beth's experience was less glamorous: cardboard boxes, duffel bags, and a lot of tears.

She had been struggling with the third load to her car when Tony had grabbed her in the kitchen. Not hard, but he had a hold of her arm in a way that made her aware that he was bigger than her.

"You want to have kids, don't you?" he had asked.

She nodded, unsure of what to say.

"Well," he had said, letting go of her. "Then, that's something you should think about."

"What?"

"You should think about that. You're not as young or as pretty as you were when we first got together. You may not find anyone else, and so you may never have kids."

Beth stood there, stunned. Suddenly, the box felt light in her hands. "Wow," she had said. She couldn't remember what else she had said, but she remembered saying wow.

"Why did we leave?" Jonah asked.

His question brought her back to the present. "Well," she said. "I didn't need to hear more. Did you?"

Jonah frowned.

"Are you going to skip class again?" she asked her son.

"Probably not," Jonah answered.

She thought of his perfect baby cheeks, his perfect baby cries, his perfect baby skin. She smiled. What a beautiful baby boy he had been. What a beautiful young man he was now.

"Okay, then. That's that. It's over. Let's go home."

"Okay Mom," Jonah said, chuckling. "Let's go."

THE ONLY PRIVATE PLACE

July 2000

When I began dating Jason, I was a virgin. So was he. The closest he had come to having sex was making out with an Austrian girlfriend who only wanted to kiss without her shirt on. It was odd, he'd told me.

I wondered if that was something European people liked to do because none of my friends who had gotten serious with boys had made out topless. I tried it a few times, but each time, I felt self-conscious, like he was looking at me too much. I would get cold, too, and paranoid my parents would suddenly open the door to the basement and catch us.

I hated how self-conscious I got sometimes, feeling like people were staring at me. It made me think of what Mr. Edwards said about Jane Austen and how she wrote most of her books in the parlor where she entertained and served guests. She had very little privacy. People were always around and watching her. I kept wondering how she got over that feeling. How she wrote at all.

Late at night, when I was certain nobody in the house could hear me on the phone, Jason and I would talk about having sex. Even then, I would go into the closet and shut the door to talk in the dark.

I liked to talk to Jason in the dark. Something about it made his voice clearer. I just had to make sure nobody downstairs picked up. It's logical to listen for a dial tone before making a call, but most of the time, my mother would just pick up a phone and start punching buttons. Then Jason and I would stay quiet until she perceived the silence and said, "Oh shoot, I'm sorry." Five minutes later—like clockwork—she'd come back on the line and tell me she needed to call my great-aunt or someone else. My mother was always calling ladies from church, too, coordinating meetings for bake sales and quilting bees.

My mother never listened for dial tones, but my father would, which was actually worse. Once, my father picked up the phone when Jason was asking me if I would ever want to have oral sex. He didn't ask me in a gross way or anything, but Jason was mid-incriminating sentence when my father picked up.

The code, when one of us was suddenly unable to talk because someone was within earshot was, "I'm not sure if I'll need a coat tomorrow."

I said the phrase immediately, but I'm still sure my father heard Jason's question. He hung up a second later and never said anything about it.

But five minutes later, my mother came on and told me to get off the phone because my father needed to call his golf partner, Earl.

I WAS THINKING about Jason again. I really didn't want to think about him.

I MISSED HIS LIPS more than anything. Just kissing him. Just that moment before he would kiss me, sitting on the L-shaped couch in the den when my parents thought we were watching a movie, and we were actually under the blanket my grandmother crocheted for my birthday. I always let him begin kissing me. I liked to feel him leaning in with his shoulder first, followed by the rest of his body.

He was older than me, and several inches taller. He was my first crush, my first boyfriend, my first everything.

Jason sat in front of me in my U.S. History class, and I stared at the back of his head. I know that sounds both stupid and cliché, but it was what happened.

His father had just transferred from Austria, though Jason was born in Ohio and spent the bulk of his childhood in Indiana. He was an American, but one entirely more interesting than the rest of us who'd been born and had grown up in the same Michigan town. I'd never even been outside of the United States, except for the time my parents took me and my cousin Christian to the Ice Capades when it came to Toronto.

Every girl I knew thought Jason was incredibly attractive. He was tall, albeit a little lanky—but at five feet ten inches tall, I was pretty gangly myself.

Sitting behind him, I did stupid things like laugh too loudly. I cared way too much about my appearance, spending ten minutes in the bathroom before second period, perfecting my eyelashes with the mascara I purloined from my mother. I would feel nervous the whole class, as though Jason—not Mr. Welter—was the one about to call on me. As if I were learning as much as I could about Jason instead of the American Civil War.

Jason was frequently out of class, though—always for cool reasons: the baseball team had an out-of-town game (he was on varsity as a freshman); the forensics meet was in Lansing; or the moot court was holding an extra practice. It didn't even matter that he missed class, though. He seemed to know everything about history. Normally, nerds like my friends and me are not that cool. But Jason was handsome enough and athletic enough and wonderful enough to transcend that; his intelligence was charismatic, enviable.

I always wanted to be around him.

I SAT IN THE BACK of the Buick, my feet crossed on the armrest between the driver's seat where my mother sat, her mother next to her. It was hot in the backseat, and my bare legs kept sticking to the leather.

My grandmother moved her hands to pat my feet and let her left hand linger on my foot for a minute. I thought it might have been awkward or uncomfortable for her to have her hand there. But it didn't seem to bother her, and I realized *I* was the one feeling awkward about it.

I thought maybe she didn't mind my feet because I only saw my grandmother twice a year—Thanksgiving and Easter; this trip to Savannah was an unexpected result of my uncle's untimely death.

It was really strange to think about Uncle Larry being dead. I realized that if anything, I should have been thinking about my uncle during this long drive. I didn't know how much I was supposed to be thinking about Uncle Larry and grieving him; however much it was, though, I was falling short.

My father couldn't come with us to the funeral because he couldn't take the week off work. I wished he'd come with us.

I couldn't think about Uncle Larry being dead. My mother kept saying that he was way too young to everyone she phoned. Uncle Larry had been diagnosed with leukemia. My mother kept telling people he should have taken himself to a doctor sooner than he did. Aunt Kathi said he'd had a persistent, awful feeling.

"You can't just *ignore* that," my mother had said to my grandmother.

"No, no you can't," my grandmother had agreed.

My grandmother nodded off a few minutes after she finally removed her hand from my foot. I was glad because my foot was starting to sweat under her hand.

She slept with her head tilted back against the headrest. I could hear her snoring in the front seat. I looked at my mother to see if she noticed the snoring. If she did, she gave no indication of it, but instead drove with her eyes straight ahead. I looked past her hands to the speedometer. She'd been driving a safe sixty-five since southern Ohio. Cars and trucks kept passing her on the left. One semi even passed us, though I realized, looking up from my reading, that it was only a trailer-less cab.

When I wasn't reading, I looked out the window at the landscape as it blurred from distinguishable objects to just blocks of the color green. For the past few hours, we'd been weaving in and out of states. I kept forgetting where we were. When we passed into Indiana for the first time yesterday, my grandmother excitedly patted my foot. A few minutes later, though, we were back in Ohio, and ten minutes after that, back in Indiana, restlessly snaking in and out of the Midwest.

Tuesday night, the three of us had gotten a hotel room, and I was forced to listen to rhythmic, seventy-six-year-old snores for several hours before finally falling asleep. I wasn't sure how much sleep I'd actually gotten. At six a.m., after listening to hours more of uninhibited snoring, I'd gone into the hotel lobby to read James Joyce and the newspaper, and drink complimentary coffee from a little blue cup so small I had to refill it four and a half times, until I got the impression that the clerk was staring at me from behind the front desk.

The night clerk kept trying to start conversations with me. "Should be hot today," he said. "Sure has been a long night," he tried again. He seemed harmless, and he was even somewhat cute without his glasses. But I realized my nightshirt was see-through and my boxers threadbare flannel. I got an awful bout of self-consciousness. I returned to the hotel room to find my mother and grandmother still asleep, my grandmother still snoring.

Quietly I slipped into the bathroom, locking the door behind me and turning on the hot water. I used the entire small bottle of bubble bath provided by the hotel.

Esther Greenwood from *The Bell Jar* said the only thing that made her fresh and new as an infant was a hot bath; after a soak, the world made sense again in light of her clean perspective.

Jason.

I sighed.

Why did it still hurt this much?

THE MOST PATHETIC THING I did to get Jason's attention: I joined the Model United Nations team because I overheard Jason tell Mr. Welter he was interested. Mr. Welter grinned and told him when and where the first meeting was. I tried to act surprised to see Jason there.

"It's Robin, right?" he asked.

I turned fifteen shades of red. The only other time I'd blushed this badly was when Mr. Welter had asked me to briefly tell the class the primary cause of the Civil War, and I had answered, staring at Jason's neck, "Because the colonists were tired of Britain's control."

"Yeah," I said, smiling.

He sat next to me and asked me to be his partner.

I couldn't believe it. "Sure," I said, my smile growing. "Which country do you want to represent? Do you have one in mind?" I glanced nervously down at the list of possible countries.

"Liechtenstein," he said.

"Oh cool," I said and nodded. "Very cool."

He laughed when I didn't say anything else. "You have no idea where that is, do you?"

I froze.

"Don't worry about it," Jason said easily. He sat back in his chair, extending his legs and crossing his feet at the ankles. He was so cool. "It's this itty-bitty country scrunched in between Switzerland and Austria. Literally scrunched in there." He pushed his hands together to show me how his crowded knuckles could represent geography.

I stared at his hands because they were easier to look at than his face.

"Pretty much nobody knows where it is. It's something like sixty square miles. I only know about it because it also borders Austria. One prince like, owns the whole country… A constitutional monarchy, I think it's called. It'll be really easy to represent because all you have to do is decide whether or not Switzerland would like whatever it is you're talking about, and then you know how Liechtenstein would feel."

"Okay," I said.

Talking came easy for him. I never talked to anyone in classes, except the friends I'd had since the third grade. It seemed like everyone in school knew him; walking down the hallway with him between classes or during lunch, seniors from the varsity team would high five him, tell him his swing was improving. For some reason, Jason seemed to *want* to talk to me.

Nobody else in my class had ever been to Europe, let alone lived there. I asked my friends Chelsea and Melanie if they knew where Liechtenstein was, and they had no idea. After the first Model UN meeting, I rushed home to look up Liechtenstein in the encyclopedia, avoiding nosy questions from my mother about how the first meeting went. I read the entire entry twice. I had to laugh when I read the section about main goods exported: ceramics and artificial teeth.

We had our Model UN meetings every other Wednesday at four-thirty p.m. The best part was that the meetings—which lasted only an hour—were held across town at the rival high school. That meant Jason and I traveled there together in his Volvo and usually wound up afterwards just driving around. We'd stop and get a soda, then continue driving aimlessly. He was the only freshman I knew who had his license—that alone made a lot of people think he was cool. I'd never been in a Volvo before, either.

Driving with Jason was the first time I learned how great it was to go wherever I wanted. While my parents knew I was with him, they of course didn't know where we were all the time. They just thought Mr. and Mrs. Kinsell, our advisors, filled several hours every week with intense study of international politics. And, in order to spend more time alone together, Jason and I neglected to mention to our parents that the meetings were actually every *other* week.

We'd started officially dating in November, gradually spending more and more time together. By Christmas, we were kissing all the time—with tongue. We would kiss for hours until I could no longer tell it was cold outside the car.

I blushed all the way through January and February, as we got more serious. Wednesdays were still the best times; we began to forego the sodas and just talk and kiss somewhere private.

In March, our UN team was preparing for the national conference in Washington D.C. I was excited for weeks. Jason and I would be alone.

Except that our advisors would be there, plus other student representatives from Sri Lanka, Japan, and a couple of Middle Eastern countries. They all had actual issues to deal with. The worst thing about the country Jason and I shared was that women were not given suffrage until 1984—the year before I was born.

Every night on the phone, Jason and I talked about the trip: mainly how we would sneak away for more privacy than we had ever known before. A few times, one of my parents would invade the line, and then we would quickly change the subject to something related to Liechtenstein.

"So you're saying we should focus more on relations with Switzerland than on Liechtenstein's strength as an agricultural superpower?"

It was so hard not to giggle as I heard my mother breathe. I could almost see her frowning suspiciously, carefully attempting to conceal her eavesdropping. "Well, definitely," I would answer, trying to sound intelligent. "I mean, I wouldn't really call such a small country a *superpower*, by any means, but its main goal, as far as financial stability and security goes, is to depend heavily on banking."

"I simply could not agree more."

When we thought we were safe again, we'd start talking about what it would be like to make love, how it would be special because neither one of us had ever done it before.

"Do you think we would be all right at it?" I asked him once.

"Oh, I know we would be."

I loved the way his voice got whenever he talked about making love with me. He would use that same voice when telling me how beautiful I was, or how he loved my brown hair and brown eyes.

"I want to make love to you," he would whisper into the phone. Not even so his parents wouldn't hear him; he would just whisper because he thought that was the type of thing that *needed* to be spoken so softly.

He didn't like to talk about how scared I was that I would get pregnant.

"We'll use protection," he told me, like he was stating the most obvious and apparent fact known to man.

I was scared and excited at the same time and counted down the days until the conference. Since it was held over a weekend, our team would be getting hotel rooms in D.C. the night after the event. That required permission slips from our parents that looked more like novellas. My father pored over mine after dinner one evening, and my mother pulled out her reading glasses, which she would only do when she read the Bible or *The Detroit Free Press.*

Finally, it was April, time for the conference. We left Thursday evening, meeting in the parking lot of the school to pile into the fifteen-passenger van. According to our arrangement, Jason would bring the condoms. When I saw him for the first time that night, I eyed his duffel bag, wondering where in that bag he had tucked them. We exchanged glances, but of course could not talk about making love until we were alone. Except in code.

"Did you bring the information about agriculture?" I asked nervously.

He smiled bigger than I had ever seen him. "Of course I did. I want us both to be ready to use the proper statistics as we advocate for Liechtenstein."

Driving to D.C. was awful because our advisors, the Kinsells, took turns at the wheel in order to get us there overnight. Jason and I slept uncomfortably on one of the bench seats, our arms and legs falling asleep in turns. It's difficult to be tall in confined spaces—even in big vehicles. For the four hours between two a.m. and the first signs of daylight, I let Jason sleep with his legs stretched over my lap, his head buried in a pillow against the window. His legs completely cut off the circulation in my own legs, and for hours, I could not feel half of myself. At one point, I wondered if I would ever get the feeling there back again.

I thought it was symbolic that I would care more about his comfort than my own.

That moment—that was when I knew we were making the right decision. That morning was how I knew I loved him—letting him rest like that. I loved Jason. Of course I should make love to him. Watching him sleep, my legs tingling, my eyes staring at the road in between Mr. and Mrs. Kinsell's torsos. One white line after another, like walking.

"WE NEED GAS YET?"

My grandmother's voice brought me out of my thoughts. I really, really needed something substantial to read.

"No, Mom," my mother said, tension in her voice. "We just filled up not that long ago. Remember?"

"Oh yes, you're right."

"I don't want to run out on the highway," my grandmother said. "You never know," she said, patting my bare foot with her hand. "You never know."

"Relax, Mom," my mother said.

"OKAY, AT ONE A.M., I want you to sneak out and meet me in the lobby," Jason said as we plotted over the phone the night before we left for D.C. I was in my room with the lights off and the door shut, crunched in the corner beside my desk and my bookcase. In the darkness, I couldn't read the titles of any of the books on my shelf. I could only see the vague outlines of their spines.

I didn't say anything, and after a moment, he asked if I was still there.

"Yeah," I said.

"What's the matter? You okay?"

"Yeah, yeah, I'm fine," I said.

"Are you having second thoughts?"

"No, no, I'm fine," I said.

I swore I heard a third party on the line, but it could have just been my imagination.

TODAY WAS WEDNESDAY. We'd probably get to Georgia in the early evening, though what we were going to do once we got there, I wasn't sure. The visitation was Thursday. The service was Friday afternoon. Growing up, I saw Uncle Larry even less than I saw my grandmother. I'd never even been to his house, so it was weird that I was only coming now that he had died.

In desperation for something else to think about, I picked up the book of travel essays and again tried to focus on seeing one word after another. My grandmother was snoring in the passenger seat again. Words strung together became sentences, sentences became paragraphs, and the paragraphs grew to pages. It worked. No more snoring, no more cramped back seat, no more ninety-two-degree heat.

No more Jason.

"Honey?" My grandmother's voice broke my trance. She must have woken up. I saw her struggling to turn around to look at me. The seatbelt restricted her motion, though. My mother must have noticed it from the corner of her eye because she moved her right hand from the wheel to my grandmother's shoulder.

"Yeah?" I answered.

"How are you doing?"

"I'm doing all right."

"That's good," she answered, hand on my foot again, patting. "That's good."

I looked to the rearview mirror where I knew I would find my mother's eyes. Normally, I was a pretty good judge of knowing when to talk to my mother and when to be quiet, just by the changing expression on her face. She'd put on some sunglasses, though, so I couldn't discern her mood.

"Are you getting hungry?" my mother asked.

"Yeah, sort of," I answered. "Are we going to stop for dinner soon?"

"I think we should," my mother said. "We don't want Aunt Kathi to worry about feeding us tonight."

"Where are we?"

"South Carolina," my mother answered. "How about we stop in about an hour?"

"That's fine," I said.

"Do we need to get gas?" my grandmother asked.

IT WASN'T TOO HARD to sneak out at one a.m. I was sharing a hotel room with Mrs. Kinsell and the only other girl on the Model UN team, Mia. I volunteered immediately for the rollaway because it was closer to the door. Everyone said they were so tired from the day's activities that we shouldn't stay up late. I was too, but I also felt wired, like I'd had an entire pot of coffee. I couldn't stop thinking about Jason.

After we turned the lights out, I studied the neon green digits of the clock from my cot as they moved gradually from midnight to one a.m.

Jason was in the lobby, sitting on a faux-leather couch and watching for me as I stepped off the elevator. His smile seemed to mirror my own nervous one.

"Hi," he said.

"Hi."

He didn't get up, so I sat down next to him on the couch.

It was funny, but for all the planning we had done late at night, in the dark, over the phone, we hadn't actually talked about *where* we would go, or how we would do it; sitting on the beige couch cushions, I think we both realized the impracticality of it all.

"Are you okay?" he asked.

"Yeah, I'm fine. Um, Jason? Where?"

"Yeah, I'm not sure."

I started to tear up, I wasn't sure why. I hadn't had a good idea of how it was going to happen, but I had wanted it to be good. Better than this. "I guess I just thought it would happen, if it was what we both wanted," I said.

"Yeah, me too."

"Stupid, huh? I mean, here we are. In a hotel and we can't even. . ."

He smiled and put his arm around me, noticing I was about to cry. He was wearing a white T-shirt and striped pajama pants. He leaned back in the couch, his long legs stretched out. He looked at me and whispered. "I love you, Robin. I *really* love you. You know that, right?"

And then I just smiled. "I know you do. I know. I still want to do this."

"Me too," he said. "I just wish we could get a room or something. But we can't."

We sat there for a second and I leaned my head against his shoulder. I didn't even care that the man at the front desk in the lobby kept glancing at us.

I think the first person you are in love with completely fascinates you in a way no other human ever will. I think the first person you get physically close to stays with you in a way you can't even explain. For the rest of your life, every other person you hold and kiss, you'll silently and secretly be comparing to that first person, the model. It's like your first love makes an imprint, and you judge all the others on how well they do or do not fit you like the first person did.

Jason was familiar to me in this way. I reached across him with my other hand and hugged him around his torso. I asked, "Do you have the stuff on agriculture?"

"Yeah," he said.

As much as we hated it, the only place we could think of to go was the bathroom. The hotel lobby had a huge unisex bathroom that locked. I went in, and several minutes later, as casually as possible, I imagined, Jason entered.

He bolted the door.

"Okay," he said, exhaling. "Are you nervous?"

EVENTUALLY WE STOPPED at a Pizza Hut about fifteen miles outside of Charleston to avoid crowds. Throughout the drive, my grandmother had spoken obsessively about crowds: how obstructive they are, the importance of not being in them, and—above all—how to avoid them.

I was starving by the time we actually sat down to examine Pizza Hut's laminated menu.

"Well," my grandmother said after a few intense minutes of scouring, "let's get pizza?"

Not long after we ordered, our waitress brought out our food and left us with plates, silverware, and a shaker of Parmesan cheese. "Is there anything else I can get the three of you?" she asked.

Nobody said anything or even looked at her, so I finally shook my head and thanked her. My mother took the metal triangle-shaped spatula and put a piece on my grandmother's plate, and then asked me for my plate.

I took my fork and pulled most of the toppings off. My grandmother cut up her piece with her fork and knife and my mother looked annoyed with both of us.

When our waitress came back smiling to ask how everything was, all our mouths were too full to answer. She was gone again a second later. It all made me feel really self-conscious.

I realized then that the three of us didn't have anything in particular to say to each other because we had spent the past day and a half together: I knew exactly what they had done today, when they had slept and for how long, what they had eaten, how often they had used the bathroom. I knew my mother had taken a long time picking out her clothes that morning. She'd only brought a few outfits, but she'd changed three times at the hotel, finally settling on a short-sleeved black blouse to go with her black skirt.

It was this strange kind of intimacy, knowing my mother and my grandmother. Right before we'd left, my father had commented on how we'd have three generations going on a road trip, how special that was, how I should enjoy it. *Estrogen-fest*, he'd called it.

My thoughts were the only thing my mother did *not* know about me. My mother didn't know how often I thought about Jason, or sex, or what happened in Washington D.C.

There's a part in *Travels with Charley* where Steinbeck talks about how a person's thoughts are the one area to which nobody else has complete access.

It is the only private place.

FROM THE HOTEL LAST NIGHT, my mother called my father, and I knew from her voice that she missed him.

"Mom's *Mom*," she had said, trying to laugh. "You know how she is."

My grandmother had been taking a bath, and I had been laying on one of the queen-size beds, reading and rereading the back of *Ulysses*. "Hailed by many as the greatest work of all time," it said. My eyes had traveled back and forth over those words until "hailed" started to make no sense, the way all words do when you say them over and over and over again, when you think about them too long or repeat them too many times.

I saw when she hung up the phone that my mother's eyes were red, which meant tears.

In my mind, I said:

Jason, Jason, Jason, Jason, Jason, Jason, Jason, Jason, Jason, Jason, Jason, Jason

until I could no longer connect his name with his face, until my lips felt a little numb and I could no longer think about what it felt like to kiss him, until the feeling I remembered of his arms around me felt foreign and too heavy.

I felt my own eyes get wet as I stretched out on the bed with the thin, tapestry-like bedspread, listening to my grandmother splash around in the bathtub, watching my mother thoughtfully stare at the phone.

THIS WAS NOT AT ALL how I had pictured it.

In all the books I had read, I'd never read about couples in love losing their virginities in some bathroom at a national Model UN conference.

"Maybe we should just start kissing," Jason said finally.

"Sure."

He stepped forward and we kissed awkwardly in front of the sink for a few moments, holding hands. We were right in front of the mirror, and I felt way too self-conscious. Even though we were alone in the bathroom, whenever my eyes slipped open, I could see us kissing. It was weird, especially under the fluorescent light, and especially trying to kiss quietly so that no one would hear us.

Jason pulled away for a moment, breathing a little hard. He pulled his white T-shirt over his head and then pulled his pajama pants off. He stood there in socks and boxer shorts. He smiled awkwardly and then stepped out of his underwear, too.

"What are you thinking?" he asked suddenly.

I'd never seen Jason this naked before. He looked silly, to be honest, wearing only white socks and standing on the tile. There was something really clinical about it all, as though I were a doctor, and I'd asked him to take off his clothes and don a hospital gown. It felt more like I was going to inspect him or diagnose him with a disease, instead of make love to him. With him.

"What?" he asked.

"Nothing," I said. I took a step forward to kiss him, but it felt sterile, nothing like the warm wet kisses we'd exchanged for so many months parked in his Volvo. I was thinking about how unromantic it was, how we would probably have to lay on the cold tile floor to do it.

"Do you want to take off your clothes?"

I looked down at my plaid boxers and t-shirt. I didn't know what to think or feel and realized Jason was unable to know what was rushing through my head.

"What?" he moved his hands to cover his penis, as though he was suddenly aware of his exposure. It wasn't like Jason to be this self-conscious, this unconfident.

And that was when I knew it wasn't going to happen, seeing him stand there, his hands covering his private parts, his Hanes socks with the red stripes at the toe still covering his feet.

"Jason," I started.

"What? What's the matter?"

Maybe he'd caught his reflection in the mirror and saw how silly he looked, too.

"I don't know, I just—"

But he reached for his underwear and pulled them hastily back on. He grabbed his pants and pulled them up and struggled to flip his t-shirt right side out to get it back on his body.

He wouldn't even look at me.

"Jason, please," I said, reaching for his arm. I wanted to hug him and feel his arms around me. "Please, don't be—"

He did hug me, but only for a second. Then he turned quickly and unlocked and opened the door in one motion, no longer worried, apparently, about who might see us, or how closely that night clerk was watching the unisex bathroom. Before I could move, he was running through the lobby to the main hallway, toward the stairs that would take him back to his room.

MY AUNT WORE A PETITE black dress to the funeral. Aunt Kathi was a small woman to begin with, but towering over her, I noticed how skinny she looked. She seemed really tired, too, with large circles under her eyes. I wore a simple black skirt, a button-up black blouse, and the shoes my mother specifically purchased for me to wear to my grandfather's funeral last year. They were too small, but I hadn't said anything about it.

I sat between my mother and my grandmother and watched the two of them cry throughout the service. Aunt Kathi gave a eulogy. For most of it, I looked at my feet. I wanted to take off my shoes, but I knew I couldn't get away with it unnoticed. I hid my feet under the pew in front of me and pulled my feet halfway out of the shoes to let them breathe.

They started killing me during the burial, though—the shoes.

I stood there in the cemetery between my mother and my grandmother, feeling the heels dig like an aerator into the dirt.

Aunt Kathi, who had kept her composure for most of the day, cried openly among the headstones. My mother had encouraged me to look at Uncle Larry during the viewing, but I had decided against it. I watched my mother and grandmother go up to the casket together, holding each other's arms.

I started to cry, too, when it was time to put the body into the ground. My grandmother, when she saw me crying, took one of my hands in hers, patted it fervently, and told me it would be all right. I think I made her cry harder.

"He's in a better place," she told me. "Honey, he's at peace."

But as they lowered the casket into the ground, I wasn't thinking about Uncle Larry or about how I'd never see him again, or talk to him again, or anything like that. I wasn't thinking about *Ulysses* and how I'd probably never read it before summer was over. I wasn't thinking about how my Saturday and Sunday would be spent driving back all the miles my grandmother, my mother, and I had just driven.

Instead, I was thinking about Jason's body: the way it looked that day in the bathroom—the one time I had seen it almost naked, and how I would never see him look that way again.

ANTIQUE DESK

Miriam and Jamie

"It's this ranch?"

Miriam nods. "You've been here before." Her voice from the passenger seat is quiet. She is still waking up. Mostly, she just sips coffee from her travel cup, her lips hovering at the lid like a hummingbird at a feeder.

I slow the truck, which belongs to my brother, Trevor, and nestle it up to the curb. I look over at Miriam and see she's nodding again and taking another sip of coffee. Her eyes are almost closed. Her eyelids look puffy. It's from crying.

I put the truck in park and turn the key in the ignition, quieting the engine. "I don't remember. Did he throw a party or something?"

Miriam closes her eyes and tosses her head back on the headrest. Her dark hair is pulled into a ponytail. Her skin looks dewy, and she hasn't bothered with makeup. Neither have I. It's almost six a.m.—too early on a Sunday to be doing something hard, but here we are.

"No," she says. She's reaching down to unbuckle her seatbelt. I see her chest rise under her parka, like she's steeling herself for the cold, for what we're about to do.

I exit the truck and wait for Miriam to come around to the driver's side so we can walk up to the house together.

The house is a brown ranch tucked near the corner of a quiet street not too far from campus.

"We came here for that *other* thing," she says. "Remember?"

It was in October—last Halloween, or close to it. Eric had told Miriam he was going away for the weekend, but the two of them had been fighting for a week, and something he'd said had struck her as fishy.

That Saturday, she swore she saw his car at the mall. Her suspicions got the best of her. She'd called him five times—he never answered. Then she felt embarrassed, drank too much vodka, and had me drive us to his house that night. She was convinced she would see Eric's car in his driveway that night. Apparently, he never parked in the garage, just used it for storage.

Or, she'd told me, she would see someone *else's* car in the driveway.

But that night in late October, we'd driven to Eric's house and had found nothing more than an empty driveway.

Just like this morning.

I don't relive the memory for Miriam, but I say, "I *do* remember now," as we walk up to his house, leaving footprints in the fresh snow. Miriam has jammed her hands in her pockets, and I wish I hadn't left my coffee in the truck.

It feels like we're about to case the joint as she crouches down and peels back the corner of the brown welcome mat. There is a small key under the mat. It isn't on a keychain—it's just a lonely key Miriam struggles to pick up until she rips her glove off. She stands up, pushes the key into the lock, and turns the doorknob.

"Come on in," Miriam says. She sounds bitter.

I have the same feeling I did last night when she came home from Eric's place crying, details of their fight and the words *it's over* spilling out between sobs.

I want to wrap Miriam in my arms and hug her, but I don't, because although I know she knows I love her, her love language isn't physical touch. Mine is.

"Welcome," she says. "Home sweet shit pile."

She keeps her coat on as she walks straight to Eric's bedroom. Eric is at a friend's house, according to Miriam.

In an hour, it will be much lighter outside, not to mention warmer. But Miriam had wanted to go first thing in the morning, and my brother had acquiesced with his truck till he needed it around noon.

Maybe after this, we could go back to the apartment and take naps.

Or get breakfast. More coffee. Stop at the store and buy Bloody Mary mix, eat scrambled eggs with toast.

We are only one week into our last semester as undergrads, so my plans for the day are thin: finish a short essay; call my mother. Maybe go for a run.

Without instructions regarding what to do with myself, I survey Eric's space as though it will give me more context for their break-up.

It's not too messy, I think—his kitchen.

I open Eric's refrigerator. Two white take-out containers—the cheap clamshell kind that let air in and do little to keep leftover food fresh—greet my eyes. There are six cans of Budweiser. A tub of fake butter.

I oscillate between thinking this house is actually nice and thinking this house is some kind of crime scene I'm disturbing.

Eric's countertops house the usual appliances. I spot a can opener, silver and unobtrusive. A Mr. Coffee. A toaster. There's a small table against the wall, underneath the window. It's just big enough for two chairs, and I walk over to it to get a closer look.

There's a pile of mail, unopened. I consider picking up the envelope on top, but I don't. It looks like junk, addressed to

Eric A. Anderson. I wonder what the A stands for. Eric A. Anderson. It feels light, weightless. Mostly vowels. The kind of name that feels like water.

I never actually met Eric A. Anderson. I never learned if he was cheating on Miriam back in October, and neither did she. And even though she spilled her guts last night, if someone asked me to articulate the reason the two of them had broken up, I knew I wouldn't be able to.

"Jamie?" Miriam calls.

I leave the kitchen and follow her voice down a dark hallway. We haven't bothered with the lights, and when I get to Eric's bedroom, it's no different.

Miriam has moved the desk—the one we're here for. It's a teal antique someone put on the side of Eric's street around Christmas. She'd dragged it into his place all by herself.

She's pulled one end away from the wall so it's sitting awkwardly at a forty-five-degree angle. Around his floor, there are clothes and books and folders, plus an oversize navy beanbag. His bed—a queen—isn't made, and his gray paisley sheets are in full view, which feels somehow like a violation.

I admire the desk for a second. It's lovely. There are flourishes of pink paint—fleur-de-lis—decorating the outside of the drawers. Pretty clear glass handles, too. It isn't in bad shape. I can see why Miriam had wanted to save it from the roadside, and I can see why she wanted to rescue it from her ex-boyfriend's house, too.

"You think we should remove drawers first?" I ask.

"No. I think it will go quicker if we just carry it."

This is arguable. I think I'm right about the fact that it would be easier to carry the desk sans drawers. But what I say is *okay*, and then I'm holding one end of the desk, and we're awkwardly waddling down the hallway. Miriam is walking backward; I am trying to match the stride and cadence of someone shorter, yet stronger than me.

In the kitchen, we set the teal desk down to regroup, wiggle our fingers. I open the door to the house, then we're waddling outside with the desk, a probable pair of cat burglars to any neighbors who might be watching.

Miriam freezes when we get to the part where we need to hoist the desk into the back of Trevor's Dakota.

"Lay it down on its side?" I offer. "Drawers up?"

She hesitates. "I don't want it to get dirty."

It's true that Trevor's truck isn't a paragon of cleanliness, but other than some mud dried on the black plastic lining, it's not too bad.

"Well," I say. "Hmm."

It's started snowing again, and fat flakes are falling around us, clinging and clumping together in their descent. It's going to snow all over this antique desk, since Trevor's truck has no cover for the back.

"Let's get a blanket," Miriam says.

"Or towels," I offer, thinking, *If I were Eric, which would I miss more?*

"Old towels," she says in a strike of inspiration. "He has some in the garage. Will you get them? And I'll get a garbage bag for my clothes."

It occurs to me this isn't the first time Miriam's packed her clothes in a hurry, nor the first time she's broken up with a guy she was kind of living with. I'd missed her the past few months. What had started as her staying with Eric on Saturday nights had quickly grown to her being absent most of the week. For the time being it seemed, she'd be back to sleeping at our apartment, back to sharing a bedroom with me.

And with this old desk.

"*Where* in the garage?" I ask.

We're walking back up to the house. Miriam's fists are clenched in the cold, and my own fingers feel numb as we step inside. "There's a washer-dryer," she says. "There's a thing with like a stack of towels."

I nod, but she doesn't see me; she's crouching before his sink on the hunt, I presume, for a Hefty bag.

I open the door to the garage. Immediately, I'm met with the sight of something I am sincerely and ironically not expecting, which is a car. A dark blue car—small.

And a man is sitting on its hood.

A young man in a black puffy coat, holding a cell phone.

He's looking up at me, and he looks surprised, but not shocked. His dark hair is peeking out from under a beanie. He has a smattering of facial hair and striking blue eyes. His coat isn't zipped, and I think he must be cold.

I realize he must have been in here the whole time, which feels creepy. I know he doesn't know that I looked through his refrigerator, but I feel slimy about having done it just the same.

"Oh," I say. "Hi."

"Hello," he says slowly.

He doesn't ask what I'm doing; I presume he's figured out what we are doing, or at least that I'm here with Miriam.

"Sorry," I say.

"It's okay," he says. "I told her I wouldn't be here."

Eric A. Anderson talks slowly, like he's taking his time with his words, ensuring they come out evenly. He is fairly attractive, though he had seemed cuter in the pictures I'd seen on Miriam's phone. Maybe because in those photos, he had smiled.

"Oh," I say. "Right. Yeah, we're just here grabbing that desk." I hesitate for a long second. He's still holding his phone in his hand, though he isn't looking at it. Instead, he's holding my gaze. "I'm Jamie."

"Eric."

"Old towels?" I ask. "Or like, old blankets?" I'm thankful in that moment that Miriam has sent me on this quest instead of herself. "It's snowing."

He nods and slides off the hood of his car.

It's still unclear why he's home, but I don't press. I've already seen too much of his space uninvited, and it's not really my business why he's lied to Miriam about being home.

This was the behavior she'd caught on to last fall, I think, as Eric walks over to the left of where I'm standing: Eric A. Anderson isn't honest.

He goes to the stack of black milk crates, open and filled with half-folded maroon towels next to the washing machine. I take a moment while he's digging through the towels to examine the rest of the garage. There's a workbench along one wall, and it's got a handful of tools on it, as well as a large black tarp, folded up—the kind you would use to cover a motorcycle.

Eric hands me the towels. A few are frayed at the edges as though they have been trimmed carelessly with scissors.

"That enough?" he asks.

"Sure?" I say, although I am not. How does Miriam plan to cover the desk so that it doesn't get snowed on as we drive home?

I wonder if Eric is thinking about how he's parting with these towels forever; I wonder if he cares.

The towels are stacked in my arms now, and I'm standing next to Eric. I notice he's not wearing shoes. Once his hands are empty, he sticks his cell in his back pocket and studies me for a second. I think he's trying to decide in the dark if I'm pretty. My hair is up in a messy bun and underneath my coat, I'm just wearing a black hoodie and an old pair of jeans. I hadn't bothered to shower.

Then again, maybe I'm wrong and Eric's not thinking anything at all, and I'm just standing in his garage, holding his crappy towels, unsure of what to say. *Thanks* feels right, though, so I say it.

"I have more," he says, nodding to the black milk crates.

"You have a nice place," I say, and I am not sure exactly why. Perhaps I want to offer an apology for violating his privacy.

"Thanks," he says. "I'm not home much."

"Yeah?" I realize I never asked Miriam where he works. She's only ever offered that he's still in school—part-time, in addition to working. I *could* ask him, but the energy and the vibe around him has built what feels like an invisible wall, and while I don't feel the overwhelming urge to get away from Eric, I don't want him to let me in on any of his evasions. I say, "Thanks again."

He walks over to the car and sits back down on its hood, assuming the same relaxed position as before. "And Jasmine?"

I turn around, but don't correct him.

"Are you going to tell her?"

I can't tell what's behind his smile: if he wants me to say yes, if he wants me to say no; if he wants my confidence, if he's asking for it. Or, if he doesn't care at all, and he's just curious—testing how close Miriam and I are.

It strikes me then that he *must* remember my name. I am Miriam's best friend, and she has definitely talked about me, and the odds that he'd get my name wrong—even though he hadn't been expecting to meet me—seem suddenly small.

It also strikes me that he has not asked if she's okay. He doesn't care about the towels. He doesn't care how Miriam is doing today.

And he's lied to her. How many times did he lie to her? Did he lie about big things, or just small things? Why would he lie to Miriam, ever?

"You know what? Actually, I'll take that tarp."

He looks at me quizzically but follows my gaze to the workbench.

"That tarp?" he repeats. He looks confused.

"Yeah." I walk over to the workbench and set down his towels. I pick up the heavy black tarp and hold it awkwardly. It's heavier than I thought it would be.

Eric looks sheepish, but he doesn't say anything.

With the tarp in my arms, I waddle to the door to the house. "Thanks," I say. I shut the door behind me, although not fast enough. I clock him sitting back down on the hood of his car, looking at his phone and idly scrolling it with his right hand as the door finally comes to a close.

I WALK DOWN THE HALLWAY and out the front door. I spot Miriam by Trevor's truck, and she's shoving a large garbage bag into the backseat.

She brightens when she spots the tarp. "Ooh," she says. "This is *way* better. Good work."

Together we cover the desk with the tarp as best we can, although some snowflakes have already landed on its wooden surface. Our treasure secure, I walk back to the front door and lock it. I tuck the brass key back under the mat where Miriam had found it.

Finally, we're back in the truck. I turn the key in the ignition, then fasten my seatbelt. I sneak a look at Miriam as I start to pull away from the curb. She looks exhausted still. She closes her eyes.

"Go slow," she says. "I don't want it getting damaged. Well," she adds, "no more damaged than it already is."

"Right," I say. "Don't worry. I will."

VISITOR'S PASS

Dalia told me I'd see her by her car—a white Nissan. I'd spot her no problem, she said, if I drove past the second speed bump. But I didn't see Dalia or her car, even as I slowed my Rav4 and rolled my window down. I was holding my phone when it rang.

"I see you!" she said. "I'm *waving*."

"I don't see you," I said, scanning the parking lot again. I saw a dozen cars—blue and black and white, a green minivan. I saw no people. What I did see from the parking lot was the beach nestled alongside the manmade lake. I could see that. I told her as much.

"I'm here," she said again. "God. I can't wave anymore."

"I still don't see you." No short woman with dark hair. No signature tan. It was fake, but she preferred I not say that.

"Are you *here*?" she asked. It was just after eleven. I wondered if she was with Ben, in the parking lot, or if she'd left him on a towel on the beach.

It was possible I was in the wrong parking lot. Club West had three entrances. It was also possible Dalia wasn't in the parking lot she thought she was in.

She could also be lying.

It wouldn't have shocked me to learn that she was sitting with her son Ben on a beach towel, her feet in the sand, her phone to her ear, putting me on. It's a bit messed up to think your friend could lie to you, but stuff like that happened with Dalia sometimes, though usually only when she was drinking.

"I went past the second speed bump, like you said. Where is *here?*"

I wasn't helping, but neither was she. It was like that with Dalia, too.

The text I'd woken up to said that she was taking Ben swimming at this fancy health club on the west side. I'd need to take the highway, which she knew I hated, but I should join her. I wasn't working Saturday. She had something she wanted to talk to me about. We'd order cherry freezes at the concessions stand and then add some Jack—no one the wiser.

We wouldn't even pay to get in, she said. She would tell the attendant she wanted to check the place out—the health club and its small adjacent beach. Pilates classes. Hot tubs and saunas. Cucumber water. It was expensive, but Dalia knew someone who told the attendant they were considering joining, and they didn't have to pay fourteen dollars for a visitor's pass.

"I don't understand where *you* are," I said, finally. I put my car in park under the biggest tree I could find in the parking lot. The yellow lines on the black asphalt were nice—clean, bright. Newly painted. The trees were lined up perfect as sentries. This was no accident; these trees were meant to welcome you. They were just one of the perks you paid for if you could afford a membership. The monthly fee was a triple-digit number. I could never afford to belong to a place like this, even if it was closer to my apartment.

Neither could Dalia.

She sighed. "Jesus, Christine," she said. "Just park. Come find me."

I locked the Rav4 and tucked the keys and cell into the side pocket of my giant tote. I hoped the canvas would be enough to keep my phone from overheating. Already, it was hotter than the forecast had called for. It might hit ninety degrees before lunch. My beach towel, sunscreen, extra shorts, and water bottle felt heavy in the bag, awkward at my side.

The part of my flip flop that divided my big toe from the rest of my toes was starting to rub at that skin, but as soon as I hit the sand, I took them off. Dalia once said a flip-flop was like a thong for your foot.

Finally, I spotted her laying on a towel in her pink-and-white-stripe bikini. Large round sunglasses covered most of her face, and it wasn't until I got close enough for Ben to wave at me that I realized her eyes were closed.

"Here you are," I said. Ben was dumping sand onto his towel. For a long moment, I studied his torso, which was equal parts muscle and chub. His hair looked wet. One tooth was missing from his smile. I was glad I had come.

"*Finally,*" Dalia said, sitting up, resting her weight on her elbows. She was trying to keep her stomach flat, I thought. "What took you so long?"

"I had trouble finding you," I said, keeping my voice cheerful for Ben. I hadn't seen Ben in a few weeks. I'd babysat for him one night when Dalia wanted to go out.

"Well, you're here now," she said, patting the sand beside her like a couch cushion. "Sit. You remembered to tell them you were thinking about joining?"

I nodded, reaching inside my bag for my beach towel. I fluffed it out in the breeze and laid it down as perfectly as I could next to her. Dalia told Ben to try not to get so much sand on his towel, but he just laughed and made a pile on hers instead.

"Here," Dalia said, sitting up all the way. She reached into her bag and pulled out a small silver vessel—not a curved flask, but one of those water bottles that held cold or hot drinks. She handed it to me, and I took it without thinking.

"I want some," Ben said.

"No, no," Dalia said. "It's not for kids. It's for Aunt Christine."

I looked at her, frowning, thinking about her cherry freeze idea. It wasn't that I was opposed to drinking, but it wasn't the case that I wanted whatever was in this flask right now.

"But I'm *thirsty*," said Ben, at Dalia's side. He was looking at me with his brown eyes. Dalia was frowning at him. I gave the bottle back to Dalia.

"It's not water, buddy," Dalia said, taking the lid off. She took a long drink, replaced the container's lid, put it back into her bag with a shrug.

"What is it?"

"Never you mind," Dalia answered, playfully touching Ben's nose. He didn't smile, though. "Go," she told him. "Go back into the lake with the other kids. There's lots of water in there."

"I can go get him something to drink," I said after Ben was out of earshot. He'd taken his yellow pail and started to walk down to the water's edge. There were about a dozen kids in the water up to their knees or their waists, laughing, splashing. The bravest floated on their backs, their stomachs, giggling each time they emerged like it was a miracle to breathe again. "You said there's a place to get food and drinks inside, right?"

"Yeah, sure," she said. "When he gets back. I want to tell you something first."

Sitting cross-legged on my towel in my one-piece, I told her to go ahead.

"So, you know that guy I went on that date with last month?" For just a moment, I got a flash in her brown eyes of how much Ben looked like her when she was happy. He didn't look much like his dad. "Well, like, two weeks ago? And more like two dates."

"Remind me," I said. I could feel a bead of sweat starting to form on my hairline. I wished for a better breeze. And that I'd peed before I'd left my apartment.

"Ty," she said. "The one I went to that concert with?"

"Right. Downtown."

"Yeah. Well, he turned out to be, like, a psycho."

"He *was?*" I asked. My surprise was sincere. She'd texted me a series of screenshots from their conversation about how much he liked her, and I tried to mentally scroll through my memory as though it were the phone in my bag, trying to read our text conversations in reverse. She'd sent me a photo of him, too—a screenshot of his dating app profile. He had red hair. Cute, kind of.

"Yeah," she said. "He ghosted me, like the day after I went to his work, you know—just to say hi. Whatever, he was a psycho. Fuck him. He's not what I want to talk about."

She reached back into her bag and took her drink out again. This time I felt like I had to take a sip, so I did—the smallest thimbleful I could manage without being obvious. It was whiskey. I would have rather had that cherry freeze, or maybe an iced coffee. As she tossed it back, I looked up at the water and scanned the horizon until I found Ben, bending over at the waist, his hands in the water.

"Spill it," I said, when I realized she'd been holding silence to add to the suspense.

She grinned. "Well, he has a friend—Kyle. He met us at the bar after the concert and I thought he was hot but, you know, didn't think much of it. Anyway, I texted Kyle when I realized that Ty was ghosting me—just to ask him like, what the fuck, you know—what the hell was wrong with his friend? And we just—I don't know, we got into this whole conversation about what *was* wrong with Ty. And Kyle was just—he said the sweetest things to me—like, that I am so hot and Ty must be nuts. And that Ty has flaked on other girls, which made me feel better. This is just Ty's MO. I'm going out with Kyle tonight. Let me show you his picture."

She reached back into her bag again to fish out her cell phone. "It's so hard to see," she said, cupping the phone with her hand.

I let my eyes drift back to the kids in the water, a few adults milling around, too. Once again, I found Ben. From the backside, he looked more grown-up than a six-year-old, and I thought to tell Dalia that, but I didn't. I didn't think the observation would make any sense outside my head. He just looked bigger, somehow, more like a little man than a boy. It must have been his trunks—blue with yellow stripes down the side. I had noticed they were falling down a little, too, so I could just see the top half-moons of his butt. He looked back at us, trying to get Dalia's attention. But all he got was me. I gave him my widest smile and waved my arms at him until he smiled back.

"Jesus," Dalia said. She was still staring at her phone. She hadn't shown me anything, so I was still waiting.

"What?"

"Fucking Jacob," she said.

"What?" I repeated. Jacob was Ben's dad. We'd all been together in high school but now that he and Dalia split, I only heard the not-so-nice things about the boy I had Chemistry with. Felt like a long time since we all went to Prom together in a big group.

The beads of sweat on my forehead were starting to trickle down to my eyebrows. I considered getting into the water. That would cool me down, although it might also remind me how badly I needed to pee.

Dalia cursed again, and then the phone was at her ear. "Jacob," she said. "What do you mean about next week?" A pause. "No, your text doesn't explain it." Another pause. Dalia stood up. She looked angry. There was sand on her tan legs, and some by her belly button, but she stood there staring at the water, listening, her sunglasses back over her eyes.

"No," she was saying into the phone. "Nope. Not okay."

That's when she turned her back to me and started to walk toward the clubhouse, the phone still up to her ear. I watched her for a minute, but she was too far away for me to hear anything.

I sighed, smoothed out my bathing suit. I was struck again by how pretty she was. It was nearly impossible to tell she'd had a kid. She'd tried last summer to get me into a bikini. She'd taken me bathing suit shopping, told me not to be so self-conscious. Even with her assurance that the fluorescent lights of the dressing room were unkind and that *of course* the high-waisted bottom looked bulky over my own underwear, I thought there was no way I'd wear anything so skimpy in public. I couldn't pull it off like she could.

I grabbed my phone from the bag's side pocket, performing a rote skim through the five apps I looked at all the time—Instagram, Twitter, TikTok, Facebook, then email. I didn't even read, just let the first post from each feed burn into my retinas. It was hard to read in the glare anyway. I was surprised the service was so good here; did Club West have outstanding Wi-Fi? Was I connected? I frowned and looked at my settings, then pulled my sunglasses off my face in hopes of seeing better.

It wasn't like I was expecting to hear from anyone. No boyfriend. No DMs. No texts. There was Cameron—a guy I had gone on a few dates with a few weeks ago, but he'd stopped texting. He'd ghosted me, I guessed. I opened my phone again. I could check his IG, see what he was up to. He had unfollowed me. I hadn't thought about him in a few days.

I let my phone fall onto my leg. I shouldn't look at his posts. It didn't do me any good—wouldn't do me any good. I knew that. I'd seen a post on Instagram that morning that said something along the lines of *let go of anything that no longer serves you*, and it'd made me think about Cameron, and the guy I dated before him, too.

Then, my next thought was about how long it had been since I'd last seen Ben.

I stood, one foot going immediately into the hot sand. I put my hand above my eye to shield my view. He couldn't have gone far.

No Ben. I didn't see his blue shorts, his black hair. Quickly, I cast a glance over to where Dalia had started walking, but she was no longer in sight at all.

I took a breath and looked back at the shoreline. Wasn't I being silly? He was right there—he must be.

I threw my phone into my bag, not caring that it wasn't in its side pocket. I didn't see Ben. I didn't see him in the water. I didn't see him bending over or sitting on the beach. I started walking quickly to the edge of the lake, my eyes sharpening on all the bodies—dads and moms, boys and girls, babies in floaties. No Ben.

Calm down. Start again. Just like in the parking lot. No white car. Dalia said she was standing there, waving. You must have missed her. You must be missing Ben.

I started at the left of the lake and assessed each body, one by one, as calmly as I could.

No Ben. Not Ben. No Ben. Not Ben.

I had made a full scan by the time I reached the water—all the way to the right of the gaggle of swimmers. Where was Ben?

"Ben?!" I called out. Two parents near me looked at me. "I'm looking for Ben," I said. "He's—he went swimming."

They looked at me, and then around in the water. I had by this point waded up to my shins. The water was freezing. I waded in until it was past my knees, and my heart was pounding. I considered diving under the water, getting it over all at once, but where was I swimming to?

"What's he look like?" the man near me asked. A boy with blue floaties hung on his leg.

"Um," I said. "I—dark hair? Blue suit? Trunks. He's—He's gotta be around here somewhere," I said. How could this be happening? This beach wasn't even big. This beach was man-made. This beach cost $129 a month to access, and each of these people were paying it, and couldn't they—was there not a lifeguard? Wasn't there—

"Is that him, hon?" the woman next to me said, pointing now. I looked in the direction of her finger. About ten yards away, out in the water, was Ben's head, bobbing up. Experiencing the miracle of a fresh breath of air. He was grinning at me. No sign of panic, no distress.

The whole thing was over in ten seconds—maybe fifteen. Twenty tops. Anyone watching from the beach would have barely registered it happened it all.

"Oh my God," I said, breath entering my lungs again. "Yeah. That's him. Thanks."

She smiled at me. "He's a good swimmer. He was really kicking out here."

"Yeah. Thanks," I said again. I was taking big strides through the water now. It was almost to my ribs.

I turned back to look at the woman, then the man. I didn't think that they were together—they seemed to be tending to different children. Everyone else seemed to be having such a good time. "We've been practicing," I said, right before I was far enough away from the mom that I would need to shout.

I'd tell Dalia about this when we got back to the beach. She'd be there, waiting, on her towel, maybe with a juice for Ben. She'd tell me what Jacob had said. I wondered if he was bailing on the camping trip he had promised to take Ben on, and for Ben's sake, I hoped that wasn't the case. I'd tell Dalia about how far out into the lake Ben swam. I could leave out the rest. I could leave out how I should have been watching him better, but also leave out that she should have done better by Ben, too. That she should have done better by me. Maybe she'd have cherry freezes—one for me, one for her. We'd put in the Jack, and the rest of the day would go just fine.

"Ah," the mom said, loudly, nodding. "Well, he's a great swimmer," she repeated.

I smiled and let the cold water wash over me, all the way to my neck as I reached out both arms for Ben, under the water's surface, two slim white ghosts in the waves that made him squeal in delight when I finally touched his skin.

ARRANGEMENTS

Carol closed the microwave door and quickly surveyed the kitchen. It was looking better. It needed to. She was about to entertain. That morning, her plans for the evening had included popcorn and red wine. Watching a movie. Maybe taking a long, hot bath.

But when Shaylin caught wind of these plans, she had insisted on coming over at seven.

Carol walked a few steps to the wine rack and selected a bottle of Cabernet—the one with the rooster on the label. She liked that one.

So what if Shaylin sees I've already opened it, Carol thought. Shaylin was cool.

Too cool. Shaylin was twenty-five, maybe twenty-six. Old enough to be her daughter, had Carol and Gerald been able to have children. *Too young to be hanging out with a middle-aged wino like me*, Carol thought, pouring the wine into a glass, then pouring another large slug before setting down the bottle.

She took another swipe at the kitchen counters, tidied the throw pillows on the couch, and straightened the remotes on the coffee table. She sprayed Febreze in the guest half bath, then lit a candle in a burst of inspiration.

Oh, what the hell, Carol thought. She went down to the basement and retrieved a handful of the scented candles she often bought in sets of five, when they went on sale at Target. The candles looked more expensive than they were, which is why she favored them. They carried semi-exotic names: Seashell Beach, Lavender Honey Parade, Fresh Snow Falling. Her favorite: Late Autumn Leaves.

Creative, she thought as she placed three candles in a row on the mantle. These unique names were probably the work of some candlemaker—rather, a marketer, making the candles seem all the more glamorous.

You can change a label or a name, Carol thought, *but the thing itself is nothing new.*

She spent a few minutes turning the lamps on and off, on and off, trying to get the lighting right. Not so bright there's a glare on the TV if Shaylin wants to turn it on.

Gerald, her husband of many years, hated the lamps in the living room. He preferred to watch TV in the den, which was downstairs.

Well—sort of downstairs. Their home was a split level, which Carol hated.

"I feel like as soon as I walk in the door, I have to decide if I want to go upstairs or downstairs," she had told Gerald many times.

"What's wrong with that?" he would reply. "Pick one."

Carol thought she heard her phone vibrate on the kitchen counter. She walked back into the kitchen and unlocked her phone, wanting to make sure it wasn't Shaylin.

When the screen brightened to life, though, there was nothing there. No missed calls, no missed texts. Nothing.

Gerald's last text to her, she realized, was from three days ago. It was a text telling her he wouldn't have time to call. He was headed to a meeting. They hadn't spoken on the phone since he left ten days ago. He hadn't even texted to let her know he'd made it safely to San Francisco.

Can't talk, the text said.

Carol poured herself a second glass of Cabernet. 6:42 p.m. She was having no trouble with the wine. It tasted so refreshing after a long day at the bank.

Fridays were the worst. Fridays were pay days, and the throng of people rushing in the door at 5:10 p.m. made Carol feel hostile. They stood in line texting, impatiently shifting their weight, staring at the large clock on the wall as though it were her fault so many people wanted to take out cash.

And the number of people who didn't seem to know a thing about their own banking disgusted Carol.

"What's your account number?" she would ask.

A customer would stare at her blankly, maybe pull a card from a wallet.

"You mean this?" he would say.

She would have to smile, sigh inwardly, and explain to the person the difference between a debit card and a banking card.

Although, Carol thought, perhaps it wasn't all their fault. Accounts could be quite confusing. There were so many account numbers and logins and passwords.

Carol managed all their accounts—hers and Gerald's—so Gerald could focus on work. Carol managed the bills. She didn't balance the checkbook the way she grew up watching her mother with a calculator once a month at the kitchen table, but she logged in to their various bank accounts and investment portfolios every few days to make sure things were running smoothly.

Carol had the sense that Gerald had no idea how long these seemingly easy tasks took. He thought she was a natural choice for those chores since she worked as a bank teller—rather, as a customer service representative. Recently, corporate had done some re-branding at the bank. It was meant to make employees more approachable, but she still had the same exact job as before.

You can change a label, but the thing itself is nothing new.

The bank hadn't exactly been her dream job. Rather, it was something she thought she would do until she could be a stay-at-home mom. That hadn't worked out so well.

When she'd hinted to Gerald that she'd like help managing their online accounts, Gerald had said, "but you're so good at it."

It seemed like a bad thing to be proud of being skilled at. She didn't disclose to Gerald how many times she accidentally locked herself out of accounts. It was so confusing. Sometimes a username was your email, but sometimes it was a unique word—or not even a word! A series of letters, numbers, and special characters—but not an exclamation point! Lately, no one wanted *that* special character anymore, so her clever username of CarolBells62! was often rejected.

The *Carol* was, of course, her name. The *Bells* referred to an inside joke between her and Gerald. When they first met at a party—one of her very first college parties—the music had been so loud, and Gerald so intoxicated that he'd misheard her.

"Carol Wells," she had said.

"Carol *Bells*? Like Christmas! You're beautiful like Christmas! Carol Bells!"

She'd been too shy to correct him. Plus, being compared to Christmas—that was the kind of compliment she used to get from Gerald.

Not so much anymore.

Carol used to make such a fuss whenever Gerald traveled for work. She'd wake up early, make him a big breakfast. Slip a love note into his luggage.

Not so much anymore.

The room that Gerald used as his home office was supposed to be a nursery. But it had only ever been a depressing, tiny workspace with twin windows and a closet. The clock on his desk read 6:58.

Carol wondered again why Shaylin wanted to hang out with her on a Friday night.

"It'll be so fun!" Shaylin had squealed. "I want to just chill out and play with your cat and paint your nails and gossip."

There was little chance their party would make it into Gerald's office, but Carol tidied it anyway. Maybe Shaylin would want a tour. Papers populated Gerald's desk, which she had been using this week while he was gone.

Carol's latest project: real estate listings. On the couch with some wine and her iPad, she surfed Zillow.com. She saved listings she liked and printed them on Gerald's printer. She'd like to live downtown. Get a place—maybe a condo?—with a better layout.

She'd casually mentioned the idea of selling their house and moving to Gerald a few times, but so far, he hadn't bitten. She needed to wait until Gerald was in town for a few days so they could look at listings together. He'd just been gone so much lately. This current trip he was on was supposed to be one of the last. Gerald said he was tired of hotels, long flights, and long meetings.

Carol wasn't sure if she believed Gerald, though; he never seemed sad to go, and he never seemed all that happy to return.

Carol heard then doorbell. She tossed back the rest of the wine, then impulsively shoved the empty glass into the filing cabinet. She smoothed her tongue over her teeth, hoping they weren't maroon.

She anticipated the next few minutes: giving Shaylin a tour, listening to her compliment the décor, watching her try to wrangle their high-maintenance Persian, Duchess. Carol took a deep breath and then on a total whim—or maybe it was the wine—she took the folder of real estate listings back out of the drawer and laid it front and center on the desk.

Let Shaylin see, she thought. *Let her ask.*

PREDICTABLY, SHAYLIN'S FAVORITE part of the house was the kitchen. It was everyone's favorite. An *entertainer's* kitchen: an induction stove, a large island in the middle. Next to the large fridge was a walk-in pantry where Carol shelved all the dry goods. All the necessities were neatly organized, labeled, ready for use. There was a long counter, too, with a bar.

Shaylin had brought a bottle of white wine, which Carol hadn't expected.

Carol suddenly remembered she hadn't eaten anything since lunch. The Cabernet was making her feel heavy. She opened Shaylin's bottle and poured two glasses anyway, as Shaylin made a toast: "To girls' night!"

Hastily, Carol found a box of crackers in the pantry. From the fridge, she pulled a block of sharp cheddar and a tub of garlic hummus. She was thankful to see the carrot sticks and green bell peppers she'd sliced.

While Shaylin vented about that day's annoying customers, Carol made quick work of slicing the cheese, creating a spread while Shaylin talked.

"If you'd like," Carol said, concentrating on keeping her knife steady, "I have frozen pizza."

"That sounds awesome. I'm supposed to run tomorrow, and I know I should be eating super healthy, but all I want is carbs. And cheese. Cheese is *so* good."

Carol smiled. She felt relief she could cook something substantial—something to help soak up all the wine. She didn't want to be drunk. She didn't want to look like an old fool in front of Shaylin.

Carol thought not for the first time that if she had had a daughter, she'd like one to be like Shaylin. Smart, beautiful, funny, bubbly. She was so cheerful at the bank. Carol didn't know why she worked there. There was no way she would stay. Shaylin took classes off and on at the community college in business—or was it finance?

Either way, once Shaylin got her associate's, she'd probably go on to a four-year university. She *should*, anyway. She was too good to be a bank teller.

Err—a *customer service representative.*

"I'm hungry all the time," Shaylin said.

"Me too," Carol answered warmly, "but I can't justify it like you. It's not because I'm training for a half-marathon, it's because I'm old and fat." She laughed.

"Oh, come on," Shaylin said, dipping a carrot stick into the hummus. Carol pre-heated the oven to 425 and removed the pizza from its thin cardboard shell. "You look great."

"For my age."

"Come *on*," Shaylin said again. "Don't be one of those ladies who doesn't know she's pretty."

Carol laughed, taking a sip of the white wine. It tasted good after all that red. It tasted light and airy—like Shaylin. Was this her fourth glass, then?

"I have an idea," Shaylin said. "Let's go play in your closet while the pizza bakes."

Carol studied Shaylin and the smile playing on her lips. She had her eyebrow pierced, which Carol usually didn't like on women, but it looked great on Shaylin.

She looked so artsy. She was wearing a black t-shirt dress over some leggings and the cardigan she had worn to the bank that day. She wore two long gold necklaces. Teal eyeshadow covered her lids. She had a wristwatch on that looked like a man's—large and gold and clunky. But it all worked, and Carol thought if she was going to take fashion advice from someone younger, she could do much worse than to take it from Shaylin.

"No," Carol said. "I just have middle-aged lady clothes," she laughed. "Black pants? The kind with the hidden panel to hide my tummy?" She put her hands on her midsection, which was flatter and firmer than many of her peers'—or so Carol thought. Of course, many women her age had given birth.

Shaylin stood up from the bar stool. "That's it. We're going to come up with at least five outfits. Come on, I do this with my friends all the time. We'll take pictures and then you'll have ideas for next week and you won't have to think about what to wear."

Carol shook her head once more before relenting.

A wave of relief washed over Carol as Shaylin marched right by the spare bedroom—the bedroom Gerald often slept in when he was home. He said it was quieter in the spare bedroom, and that he'd grown accustomed to sleeping alone. She had made that bed, ushered his dirty laundry from the floor to the bathroom hamper anyway.

Shaylin cut a path straight to the primary bedroom, found the walk-in closet immediately, turned on the light, and surveyed Carol's wardrobe. She invited Carol to pull her favorite pieces of jewelry and put them on the bed.

"Okay," Shaylin said. She took a long drink and rubbed her hands together. "Let's see what we're working with."

IF SHE HADN'T BEEN keenly listening for it, Carol might have missed the oven timer beeping insistently from the kitchen.

"I'll be right back," she told Shaylin, who was arranging an old suede skirt Carol hadn't worn in ages on the bedspread with a cobalt-colored blouse.

She cut the pizza into eight pieces. She was supposed to let the pizza cool and settle before serving, but Carol was having too much fun to wait. She loaded a large serving tray with plates, napkins, and half the pizza. She went to the refrigerator and pulled out a container of shredded Parmesan cheese. *What the hell*, she thought, and pulled a bottle of ranch dressing, too. She liked to dip her crusts in ranch when Gerald wasn't around.

She was about to leave the kitchen when she heard her phone vibrate on the counter. She gave it a glance. New message from Gerald. She didn't read it. *He hasn't texted in days, and he wants to text me now? When I'm finally having fun? Forget it.*

She walked back to the primary bedroom and placed the tray on the bedspread, careful not to disturb Shaylin's thoughtfully coordinated outfits. She noticed Shaylin had matched a pair of black boots with one of her favorite gray dresses—one she didn't wear often because it was wool and quite itchy. Shaylin was moving a pair of earrings from one outfit to another, looking at Carol and then at the clothes. Carol smiled.

"I need to see you in this dress with this scarf," Shaylin said. "I can't tell if the scarf is enough by itself, or if you need earrings."

Carol giggled. "Yes ma'am. You should take a break. Have some pizza."

Shaylin took a slice and chewed thoughtfully. Carol picked up the clothes and stepped into the bathroom. She decided at the last second to keep the door partly open. She was aware that Shaylin would be able to see her reflection in the mirror from where she was standing, but it felt wrong to Carol to close the door, like it would cut off the intimacy of the evening.

What twenty-five-year-old wants to play dress up with me on a Friday night? she thought again, stepping out of her black pants and pulling her sweater over her head. *Probably, she's meeting up with a boy later. Still, she's so nice to come over. Keep me company.*

Carol modeled Shaylin's first outfit cheekily, putting one hand behind her head like a pinup model. Shaylin clapped.

"Oh my God, you look great! Purple complements your complexion. Your hair is a pretty shade of brown—do you color it? You need to wear purple more. My roommate is really into dressing for your season. I should text her your picture and ask what you are."

Carol giggled again. She wanted to believe this is what having a daughter would be like, but she didn't really think it would be. Her own daughter, at this age, probably wouldn't have been interested in this. It was just a fantasy to think she would have had moments like this with her own daughter.

Suddenly, Carol felt empty. Hollow. She felt tears welling up in her eyes. She stepped away from Shaylin and back into the primary bathroom, pretending she needed the bright light and the big mirror to assess herself again. "You don't think it's too much?"

It's just the wine, Carol told herself. *Eat another piece of pizza once you get this outfit off. Don't get weepy, for God's sake. Don't make her uncomfortable. You're having a fun time—you haven't had fun like this in ages.*

"No, you look hot, Carol! You should keep your hair down with that outfit. And you *don't* need the earrings. Wear that Monday. Please?"

"Thanks," Carol said. She smiled at herself in the mirror, making sure she didn't look weepy. Her teeth looked fine. Her cheeks were pink. "Hey, and I mean it," Carol added suddenly, still looking in the mirror. "Thanks for coming over. I'm having so much fun. You were right—I needed some girl time."

Shaylin didn't say anything. Carol took another look in the mirror before stepping back into the bedroom. She found Shaylin sitting in the armchair by the bed, chewing pizza and staring at her phone. "Shaylin?"

"Oh, sorry. I grabbed my phone to text your picture to my roommate and I got one of those *New York Times* alerts."

"*New York Times?*"

"Yeah. Headlines. I started reading. There was a plane crash—a flight from California. It was a small plane, but it killed like, 137 people. Jesus."

"Oh," Carol said. Her arms dropped. She didn't think she was slurring, but she wanted to make sure. She spoke carefully, "That's too bad." She continued to stare at Shaylin, the faint glow of her phone on her face. She was so pretty. Shaylin shook her head and pressed a few more buttons.

"Okay," she said, holding her phone up to Carol. "Say cheese!"

"Cheese!"

That odd feeling was back—the one from the kitchen. *It's just the wine*, Carol told herself. Shaylin ushered her into the bathroom to try on a velvet skirt that hadn't been worn in a decade.

It's just the wine, Carol told herself again.

Carol smiled for picture after picture, focusing on having fun. She couldn't remember the last time she felt so happy.

She was an *Autumn*, Shaylin's roommate had replied.

Later that night, an hour after Shaylin had left, she finally read the message from Gerald. There had been a missed call, too—*four*, actually. She'd missed all that noise from her phone in the other room. She polished off Shaylin's white wine as she read Gerald's text.

Pick up the plane is going down say goodbye to my mom tell her I love her Carol I love you CarolBells

Carol spent the next hour in a daze, on the couch, holding her phone and her empty wine glass. At one point, she fell asleep. She woke up to Duchess meowing on her stomach at dawn. She'd forgotten to feed the cat. All day Saturday, she surfaced through her hangover and fielded dozens of phone calls in a haze.

There is so much to do, Carol thought.

Deliver the news to his family. His mother. His friends. There was the correspondence, the emails. She would need to make the arrangements.

She would need to log into all their accounts and update everything. She would need to declare him dead everywhere.

The house. She wouldn't want to stay; it was too much for a single person. She'd want to move downtown—perhaps something with a better floor plan.

Gerald had decided to take an early flight home, it seemed, and now Carol Wells had a lot she needed to manage.

PSYCHIC READING

Miriam and Jamie

She has me by the elbow. Even through the thick wool of my winter coat, her grip is ridiculously strong for someone so skinny.

That's Miriam: Popeye in Olive Oyl's body.

She's pulling me recklessly now behind a rack of women's clothing. As she does, formal gowns in stiff, beaded material drag at my arm as though trying to get my attention.

Then, Miriam's forcing me up a small set of stairs.

This is where the saleswoman told us to go.

This is the Women's Lounge. The Women's Lounge is the anteroom to the store's women's restroom.

And it's huge. There's a long pink tufted couch and a matching loveseat. A gigantic mirror adorns one wall, and under it, a ledge that stretches for days.

And a man. A man is seated behind a card table in the corner of this lounge. On the table, half a dozen candles burn.

"This is *bananas*," Miriam says.

The man smiles. He's got shaggy brown hair and light blue eyes. He's wearing a corduroy brown shirt and dark jeans. He looks young.

"Welcome. Please have a seat." His voice is friendly. I don't know if I was expecting him to have a crystal ball and a turban, but he's just a normal-looking guy.

Miriam and I sit down in the two folding chairs. We take turns shaking his hand—first Miriam, then me. As I sit, smoothing my coat under my rear, I think, *isn't this how all adventures with Miriam begin?*

The night starts out normal enough: dinner at an Italian restaurant downtown, me stuffing my tired body with gnocchi. We order a bottle of red wine. Then another.

Then Miriam pitches an idea: she's spotted a poster in the window of the restaurant advertising free psychic readings in the upscale women's boutique down the street.

"Powder?"

She nods. "Yeah. The old Jenkin's."

Jenkin's was a popular department store chain in the 1950s. The building, though, must have gone up in the 1800s. Stepping into this Women's Lounge is like stepping out of a time machine. This room—it's from a time when women needed a private space in a public place. To take off their elaborate dresses to use the toilet. To rest on fainting couches. This room is like a parlor for women out in public—a safe place to go when away from the safety of home. It's a wonder it's never been remodeled.

Evidently, to encourage holiday shopping, downtown retailers are having special store events: karaoke, photo booths, prize giveaways, gin tastings. And this one: a free psychic reading.

This is how I find myself buzzed in the middle of December in a Women's Lounge, across from a man who has introduced himself as Dirk.

"Hi, Dirk." Miriam's voice has a flirty edge. It'd come out for our waiter as well. She's taken off her scarf and laid it on the table. "I'm Miriam, and this is Jamie. She just had a baby."

"Wow," Dirk says, looking at me brightly. "Congratulations!"

"You can't tell, can you?" She's complimenting my post-baby body, which she also did at the restaurant. But it feels silly since I'm still wearing my coat. Underneath, I don't look great. It will take time for the baby weight to melt off, I know. Next to my best friend and her sharp angles, though, I'm an amorphous blob of pale blubber.

"I've got dark circles under my eyes," I joke, setting my hobo bag on the floor.

"How old is your baby?"

I'm about to answer *two months* when Miriam cuts me off. "Aren't you supposed to tell *us*? You're the psychic!"

Dirk smiles. I wonder if he can tell how much wine we've had. "I'm not a mind reader, unfortunately."

I notice for the first time a mason jar near Dirk's left elbow. It contains a handful of bills: ones and fives. Not more than thirty bucks. Tips.

"Right. You won't tell us something we already know, huh?"

He smiles. "Have you ever had a reading before?"

"I've had my palm read. And I've had an astrological reading. Is that what this is like?"

Dirk shakes his head. I wonder if there are any women in the restroom—if at any moment, a woman will come out into the Women's Lounge, wiping her hands, startled.

"I don't use astrological info, although there's merit to it. I just read people and go by feelings, you know—intuition, vibes, energy, all that kind of thing."

"So," Miriam says, "you want to see my *aura*." She's said *aura* like it's a dirty word.

I look at Dirk. He's smirking. "Maybe. Who's going first?"

The room is silent for a moment, and I study Dirk's chin. It's a good one. He doesn't have any facial hair, but a goatee would look good.

That's when I look over at Miriam and realize she's pointing at me.

"Okay, Jamie. Ready?"

Although I don't hate new experiences, like having a psychic reading by a kid who doesn't look old enough to order a drink, for the second time since we arrived, I feel pressure welling up in my breasts. I didn't bring my normal pump. Rather, I'd stuffed the small manual one into my bag. I had not been planning to use it, but I also hadn't anticipated we'd be out this late. I hadn't been out drinking with Miriam for a year. I was rusty. I should have known the night would take off on us.

"Actually, Miriam, can you go?"

I'm realizing we may only have time for one reading before I will need to pump. Pumping is still a new trick. And I've only got one container to store the milk—I should have brought two. But I'm also remembering that Miriam drove, and it would be rude to push her into driving before she's ready.

"Why?" Miriam's frowning.

"I want you to," I say, trying to give her a look I hope she understands to mean, *please.*

Miriam says, "I'm ready for my close-up," as she puts both palms up for Dirk.

Dirk gives a smirk, then closes his eyes. He takes Miriam's hands into his, holding them, rubbing his fingers over her skin.

She asks how long he's been doing this, but he just smiles. It's her cue to be quiet. I'm aware of how creepy this would be if Miriam weren't here—alone in the anteroom to a bathroom in a building that's so old, there's a zero percent chance it isn't haunted.

"So," Dirk says. His eyes are still closed. "One way I like to get started is by you telling me what questions you have."

Miriam looks at me and winks. "The usual, I suppose. *Love.* Does everyone say *love?*"

Dirk smiles but says nothing. He opens his eyes for a moment before closing them again. I bet he thinks Miriam is pretty. Everyone thinks Miriam is pretty. She is.

"Can you be more specific?"

Miriam gives Dirk a dramatic sigh. "I have this boyfriend. It's *very* off and on. *Very.*"

She's talking about Rich. Rich recently broke up with his girlfriend of over a year and immediately reached out to Miriam, which sent Miriam into a texting tizzy with me. I had tried my best to keep up with our exchanges, though it was difficult to do between trying to breastfeed, trying to sleep, trying to shower, trying to eat; and above all, trying not to kill Mike, my sweet husband, who was trying his best but seemed helpless when it came to the laundry he couldn't finish, the meals he couldn't cook, the dishes he never put away.

Many of Miriam's texts had fallen through the cracks. Sometimes, though, I would answer at two in the morning as Ethan was happily sucking away, and we'd somehow found a position in the glider that seemed comfortable for both of us.

"Do what you want," I had texted Miriam at one point. And then added, quickly, "You know I mean that in the most supportive way."

It felt strange to be texting about Rich Hooper as I was on maternity leave with my first baby. Rich had been playing with Miriam for years. We weren't in our twenties anymore. We were supposed to be done with boys who don't know what they want.

"I'm wondering if Rich should get another chance," Miriam says, raising her eyebrows. "He doesn't *deserve* one, but since the universe has a grand sense of humor about the whole thing, I'd love your take."

Dirk is quiet. Miriam is still watching him. I'm not sure what he's divining from her hands, but he seems to be thinking.

My breasts are starting to speak up. My once-stoic body was now a loud and bold one, never afraid to speak up when it wanted food, water, sleep, or to sit down. The last month of my pregnancy, my body screamed for glazed donuts and to do nothing but lay in bed watching *The Sopranos*.

Now, my body yells, *You need to feed your baby*.

I wish Miriam could read my mind. We are usually so in tune. Couldn't she divine from just a look that I wasn't game for this much longer?

"Interesting," Miriam says a minute later. With his eyes open, finally, Dirk has released her hands. He told her that while the passion with Rich is real, there aren't many indications from the universe that a long-term relationship will work.

But Miriam keeps poking holes in what he's saying, making Dirk second guess himself.

I know I'd find this more amusing if my breasts didn't feel like softballs.

"Okay," Miriam says. She's fished a five-dollar bill from her wallet and sticks it into the tip jar, for which Dirk effusively thanks her.

"Your turn."

"Oh," I start, looking between Dirk and Miriam. "You know, that's okay. I think—we should probably go."

Dirk looks hurt. I think he thinks I want to leave because he's done a bad job reading Miriam. He was counting on my five bucks, maybe.

"No, you *have* to."

"I'm sure Dirk has folks waiting," I add, although there wasn't exactly a line outside the Women's Lounge when we'd arrived. I don't add that my breasts hurt and that because my buzz is wearing off, I feel the discomfort more than I did when we first sat down.

"Come on, J," Miriam says. I know invoking my nickname is a sign she's serious. My breasts press tightly against my bra. I fight the sudden urge to cry. Again.

Ethan spit up on the only "going out" top that matched my maternity pants, so just before Miriam pulled into my driveway, I'd tearfully grabbed a thin gray sweatshirt that had been Mike's at one point. I'd cried kissing Ethan goodbye, too, handing him to Mike, who in turn had kissed me on the forehead and urged me to have fun.

"Okay. I just—I should get home soon," I say apologetically. Dirk smiles, but even in the candlelight, the hurt hasn't worn off his face. I feel terrible. "To my baby."

"I can be quick. Two minutes. Just ask me what's on your mind."

"Honestly, I can't think of anything I have questions about."

"Ten words or less. Big life changes make for great questions."

He's hinting at becoming a mom. I say okay, and Dirk brightens a bit.

"Will I be a good mom?"

Dirk smiles and gestures for me to give him my hands. I do. His fingers are long and slender. His hands are smaller than Mike's. I look at Miriam and she's texting. Probably Rich. She's probably telling him that Dirk doomed their relationship. Despite my milk ducts, I smile.

The next few seconds are a bit of a blur: Dirk's eyes close, his face changes, looking more and more concerned. I'm telling myself not to worry if any milk leaks onto Mike's sweatshirt. No one can see it under my pea coat.

Finally, Dirk opens his eyes. The look on his face is concerning. I hold my breath. I look over at Miriam, but she's still squinting at her phone.

"I'm sorry," Dirk mutters. "Jesus."

"What?"

"I don't know how to say this," he says, frowning. "I'm getting…"

"What?" Miriam presses. Her phone is still in her hand.

The smile is gone from Dirk's face. His voice is faulty when he speaks again. "I'm trying to understand what the universe is communicating through your energy, and I'm afraid it's not good. I'm seeing death in your future. A close family member. An accident. I'm seeing… It's your son. Yes. I'm seeing Ethan is dead. Jesus. I'm so fuckin' sorry."

I rip my hands from Dirk and push the cheap folding chair back from the card table. In an awkward motion, I grab my bag from the floor and rush into the restroom.

"Sorry—I need to go. Sorry." My voice breaks as I apologize.

I curse myself for caring about Dirk's feelings—Dirk, who is clearly horrible at this. He's doing it for free, after all.

I need to get away from him—this young man who has just told me my son is going to die. And I know I'm just emotional—I'm tired and I'm overwhelmed. I have to pee. I miss Ethan, his round cheeks, and my breasts hurt, and I can't take it anymore.

Inside the restroom, I'm confronted with a large space: six toilets in individual stalls. I grab one and lock the door, pulling down my maternity pants. This pair of underwear has been effectively ruined; I've stretched out the waistband and spotted blood countless times on the white cotton crotch. I don't care.

Peeing is a relief. As soon as I'm done, I wash my hands, then rush eagerly back into the same stall, sit on the lid this time. I think about how much more comfortable the plush couch in the Women's Lounge would be for this.

Women from previous centuries had it right, I think. *Privacy is everything*.

I pull off my coat, Mike's sweatshirt, and then I yank down the cups of my bra. Milk is leaking from both nipples. I start crying again. I'm digging in my bag for my pump while milk leaks onto my flabby stomach when I hear the door to the bathroom close. I feel Miriam before she speaks.

"You okay, J?"

"I'm fine," I sniff. "I'm just uncomfortable. I need to pump."

"Do you want help?"

I smile. Of course Miriam is offering to help. She would do that for me.

I secure the manual pump on my left breast and begin pumping away like a madwoman. The relief is immediate. I close my eyes, pumping and pumping. After thirty seconds, I switch and relieve the pressure in my right breast. I picture Mike giving Ethan a bottle and fight the urge to cry.

"I'll say this quiet so he can't hear," Miriam says. She's whisper-yelling at me as I pump milk into the plastic bottle. "But that kid doesn't know what the hell he's doing."

"*You* tipped him."

"He's *trying*. It's not easy. I have a cousin who does Tarot—Madeline. You remember her. She's good."

I listen to Miriam talk about Madeline until my breast feels soft again. Normal. I know she's just talking to fill the space and calm me down, and I love her for it.

The small plastic bottle is full. I feel sad. This should be for Ethan. I dump the milk into the toilet because it's full of wine and tears, and I have no idea when I'll be able to refrigerate it. The pump I stick back in my purse, not wanting to wash it in front of Miriam, even though over dinner, I told her I would show it to her.

I put Mike's sweatshirt back on, then my coat, stepping out of the stall. I find Miriam applying lipstick at the mirror. She doesn't look at me as I splash cold water on my face and take a long drink from the faucet.

"It's *shit*, okay?" Miriam says. She's still at a whisper as she throws her lipstick into her purse. "I'm sorry he said that.

None of it's true. Ethan is gonna be fine. He *is* fine. You're a *great* mom. Let's get out of here. Let's get dessert somewhere."

I follow her back into the Women's Lounge where she says a loud but polite goodbye to Dirk. I try to echo it, but I feel like I can't speak, so I just hold up a hand dumbly. I see Dirk wave, but the look on his face is as grim as it was when he'd given my reading.

Walking out of the Women's Lounge, there's no line to see Dirk. Powder seems to be thinning out. It must be closing soon.

I can't shake the feeling that neither of us will forget the time we got a free psychic reading inside a Women's Lounge, and I cut the psychic off before he could finish because he told me my baby was going to die.

I can't shake the feeling that Dirk has cursed me somehow—or that this whole adventure was a mistake. I should have stayed home with Ethan, with Mike. I should have told Miriam I wanted to go home after we split the check at dinner. I shouldn't have let her drag me here.

And I can't believe, as I recount the whole incident to Mike when I get home, how spine-tingling scared I get when I realize that at no point that evening had Miriam nor I told Dirk that my baby was a boy, or that we had named him after my grandfather: Ethan.

LOGGERHEAD

My husband Joe referred to The Lodge as *poor man's Disney World*: an indoor water park on a budget. But when the young man behind the counter at Hungry Wolf handed me a black, brick-like buzzer, which he said would light up in approximately twenty minutes when our order was ready, I didn't mind.

"If you want, you can wait at the bar," the young man said.

"Oh, thanks."

I shuffled around the tables outside Hungry Wolf, occupied by families sharing slices. Habitually, I pushed one hand into my stomach as I passed, holding it in, pressing my fingers against the terrycloth. Everyone toted the same blue and white, resort-issued, oversized towel. Underneath mine, I wore a tankini. More modest than a bikini, not as grandmotherly as a swim dress.

That was another nice thing about The Lodge: no one particularly cared what they looked like. Joe could call it whatever he wanted, but I thought it was sweet—just families, like ours, dozens and dozens of them, tucked into this resort.

The Lodge had everything we could want: Hungry Wolf for pizza, the Lickety-Split ice cream shop where we'd gotten waffle cones stacked with orbs of Rocky Road; the Aurora Borealis Arcade, where we'd spent an hour and sixty bucks this morning watching the kids' hearts break at claw machines that took their tokens and yielded no stuffed animals.

This is perfect, I thought, walking over to The Grizzly Bar—the bar attached to the family-style restaurant, Critters. The Lodge was a fantastic place to spend our long weekend. The kids were loving it. Joe was in a good mood. I'd managed to get all student assignments graded and returned Friday before we left, enjoying the feeling of setting up an out-of-the-office automatic reply.

At The Grizzly Bar, two middle-aged men and one woman occupied three of the available half dozen stools. Behind us, the soft cacophony of diners eating resort-themed hamburgers in Critters wore on. The two men were in athletic shorts and t-shirts; the woman, like me, had on a two-piece suit, but instead of a towel, she'd overlaid it with a lacy kimono. Her dirty blonde hair was in a ponytail, half-wet, lying on one shoulder. I took the seat at the bar that made the most sense—one that left one spot between me and the woman.

The bartender seemed to be MIA, so I pulled out my phone to text Joe that the order was in, and I'd be back in the room in twenty minutes. I set the buzzer in front of me at the bar so I wouldn't miss it going off. That buzzer also let everyone know why I was here: just a middle-aged woman in a damp tankini, waiting for pizza.

"Hey there." The bartender had returned. He had a thick scruff of hair and a long nose. He looked like a cousin of mine in Minnesota I was fond of. "Sorry about that wait."

"Oh, not at all."

"Get you something?"

That was the other nice thing about The Lodge: they never carded. No bartender looked at a tired mom and suspected she was trying to pull a fast one.

"White wine?"

"Chardonnay?"

"Sure," I said. "Thank you."

He was back fast with my wine and a smile. Obediently, as I had with the young man at Hungry Wolf, I offered him my left wrist, which was adorned with a bright pink band. The bartender scanned my wristband with his reader till it beeped its approval. This parlor trick let resort-goers forget they were spending money; I wouldn't notice this glass of wine cost eight dollars until we were driving home Monday and I pored over our itemized bill.

"Still cheaper than Disney," Joe would say from the driver's seat.

The first sip hit just right, and I was happy about my choice not to send Joe for the pizzas. He was in the room helping the kids take baths, getting them into pajamas. I didn't doubt they'd want to return to Aurora Borealis later to redeem themselves at the claw machines.

"Hey." The voice belonged to the woman in the kimono, and when I looked at her more closely, I realized her hair wasn't in a half-wet ponytail, it was in an elegant braid resting against her collarbone like a trained parrot. "This might sound crazy, but are you Casey Ellis?"

I blinked. "Umm," I said, "yeah. I mean, I *was*. Casey Zellner now."

"Oh my God," the woman said, shaking her head. I noticed she had a slushy in front of her—the same kind they sold poolside—the Loggerhead: frozen fruit blended with vodka. "I thought that was you!"

She looked familiar, but I couldn't place her. My hand nearly twitched with the urge to open Facebook. I was losing the ability to remember who people were without my social media rolodex: friends, students, acquaintances, playground moms, my colleagues, Joe's colleagues, my kids' babysitters. I was at a point in my life where everyone sort of looked like someone else.

The woman stood from her bar stool and moved to take the seat next to me. Instinctively, I set my phone face down next to my buzzer. At the scrape of her stool, the two men in shorts looked our way, and I couldn't help but notice one of them checking her out.

"Do you remember me?" she asked. There was a smile on her face. She set her Loggerhead next to my glass of wine on the bar, like our drinks might recognize each other.

I smiled and studied her. She was beautiful and probably around my age, but I couldn't place her. Smooth skin, arched eyebrows, long lashes. She was definitely wearing a full face of makeup. I hadn't even bothered to pack concealer, although I certainly needed it. Her eyelids were colored a nice shade of bronze, and if I wasn't wrong, she'd lined her eyelids.

I was just about to say, "No, I'm sorry," when she cut in.

"Leah," she said. "Wyland. Pepper Creek High?"

Ohhhhhhh, my brain supplied. *Yes. Right. Leah Wyland.*

I told my face to stay still. I wasn't a great actress; Joe would attest. I always thought it was a good thing I was such a bad liar, but waiting at The Grizzly Bar for two pizzas, one cheese and one with mushrooms and peppers for Joe and me, I wished I was better.

"Oh my gosh! Hi Leah. It's so great to see you! Were we—were we in the same class?" I asked. I knew we weren't.

"No, you were below me."

"Right," I said.

Leah took a long drink of her slushy. At the sound of her straw coming up empty, the bartender was in front of her, asking if she'd like another. She nodded.

"So… how are you?" I asked Leah, once our bartender, Toby, stepped away. "Do you live in the area?"

Leah shook her head. "No, I'm still in Bay City."

Our hometown. Where we'd endured four years at Pepper Creek High. Where she'd ruined my life for a bit.

"You live around here?" Leah asked. Then she chuckled as though she realized it sounded like a pickup line. The man nearest to her was looking our way, though I couldn't tell which of us he was staring at. His face was marked with tan lines from sunglasses.

The bartender returned with her drink and Leah smiled at him as he scanned her wristband—the same shade of pink as mine.

"No. We're in Kalamazoo," I said. Then I checked myself. That habit of saying "we"—sweeping Joe and the kids up with me whenever I made small talk. "My husband and I. We have two kids."

"Wow," Leah said, and I was struck in that moment by two things: she seemed actually happy for me, and that I was surprised by that.

But I shouldn't be—should I? I nodded and took a sip of wine, looking at both the buzzer and my inert phone as I set the glass down. I couldn't wait to get back to the room, hop on Facebook, read everything about Leah Wyland there was to read, look at every picture there was to see. Assuming, of course, we were friends which, I realized, I actually had no idea.

"How about you?"

"Three," she said, shaking her head. "I'm here with them. And my boyfriend. And *his* kids. Two of them."

"Oh wow. That's amazing! You guys must have ordered a lot of pizza," I joked. She didn't laugh. "That's cool," I added. I'd run the conversation into some kind of corner.

"So, what do you do?" she asked.

"Oh. I'm teaching."

"High school?"

"Community college."

"Cool. I always knew you were smart," she said, smiling. "And what do you do?"

I was more or less begging that square buzzer to explode into a fit of light and sound in front of me. I was already thinking about how I would tell Joe about this encounter, already anticipating his follow-up questions.

I'd told him about the Leah Wyland incident when we were first married, or maybe when we were engaged. We'd been having some conversation about first love. Joe thought the story was a little hilarious. In the long run, he'd said, it wasn't a big deal—just an example of how events in high school can feel momentously important, but then just aren't. By the end of my recounting, I'd realized how funny it was, too, in retrospect.

Leah shrugged. "Nothing, right now. Just the kids."

"Oh cool. They're such fun ages," I said, although we hadn't shared our kids' ages. This went unnoticed by Leah, who took a big sip of her Loggerhead, then held her glass in the air between us. I could see wrinkles around her mouth, circles under her eyes, up close. "You *really* don't remember me?" Her tone indicated I was still a bad actress, and that she might be on to me.

Of course, she also might be buzzed.

"Did we have Chem?" I asked.

"Nope."

"Shoot." I took another sip of wine—big enough to inspire Toby to start walking over. "Algebra?"

"Nope," she laughed. "You're supposed to be the smarty-pants, Ms. *Professor*." She slurred *professor* just enough to make me wonder how long she'd been sitting at The Grizzly Bar. How her itemized bill would look when she—and the boyfriend?—checked out. Then I wondered if we'd run into her tomorrow. Joe and I were planning on spending all day Sunday here with the kids, too. We'd leave Monday morning; I didn't teach Mondays, and Joe had taken the day off.

Running into the woman who had gone on an overnight youth group retreat with my first boyfriend and had made out with him in the back of the van while everyone else was asleep and apparently, the youth group leaders too focused on the highway to look in the rear-view mirror on occasion—that hadn't been in my plans for tonight.

The details were all coming back to me now: the Sunday night Logan had returned. How I'd taken the cordless phone to my room, up past my bedtime, but instead of Logan telling me about s'mores and campfires and Bible sketches, he'd sobbed and confessed what had happened with Leah Wyland—the senior who had seduced him with french kissing. He'd been stupid, he'd said—helpless. And would I forgive him? *Could* I pray about it and forgive him for being weak and cheating, for throwing our six-month relationship into the trash? For a make-out session with *Leah Wyland?*

"You need another?" Toby asked. His eyes oscillated between us.

Leah looked at me. "Say yes!"

"Shoot. I would, but this thing's going to go off any moment." I gestured to the buzzer. "The kids are starving after swimming all day."

"Oh come *on*," she said. "Let's reminisce!" That word got slurred, too.

"I wish I could, but I can't keep the troops waiting. Have you guys had dinner?"

She rolled her eyes. "I told him I needed a little time away, you know? From the circus? I think he took them for ice cream. They might still be in the water. I'll find them later. Pretty please, have another with me? It's been *ages*."

And then like a sea-parting miracle, with Toby as witness, the Hungry Wolf buzzer began flashing red, vibrating so loudly it drew the attention of the two men who had, during my conversation with Leah, each turned to scrolling their respective phones.

"Ah, drat," I said.

"Just me, then," Leah said to Toby. "This girl is no fun. Just like in high school. Goody-two-shoes. Girl Scout." Toby looked a little uncomfortable, and Leah told him she was just kidding. "Although you were kind of uptight back then," she said to me, grinning.

I forced a smile and thanked Toby. Then I turned to Leah.

"Well, it was so great running into you. Here, of all places! Maybe we'll see you guys again this weekend."

She gave me a look, moved her drying braid to her other shoulder. I could picture her making out with Logan, touching him in the back seat of that van—still, after all these years. Just like I had when I was seventeen. The pain of those months after Logan and I broke up. How it was all over school what Leah Wyland had done. How I'd endured months of people whispering about me and Logan and Leah behind my back. I swore even the teachers knew. Pepper Creek High was not a big place. Leah Wyland had made me feel like everyone felt sorry for me. Leah Wyland had made me feel like I couldn't get out of there fast enough.

I tried to picture Logan Dermont's face in my mind, but I realized I only had a dim sketch of how he used to look, how he used to kiss me. I hadn't realized how faded he was in my memory. I wasn't sure where he'd ended up, what he was doing now. People had gossiped, right after it happened, that Logan and Leah would date, but they never did. I wasn't sure if Leah refused to date him, or if Logan refused to date her. Either way, the scandal stood. They never got together, at least as far as I knew.

For a month, after it happened, Logan had begged me to take him back. I'd held strong. I'd told him no. I wouldn't let him back in.

And I'd gone out of my way, until Leah graduated that spring, to never run into her again. But of course I did, and each time I saw her, she smiled at me, smugly. She never acknowledged she did anything wrong. I'd wanted to set fire to her locker, egg her house. I fantasized about something awful happening to her, but nothing awful did. Every time I saw her, I acted like I didn't know what she'd done with Logan, what she'd done to me. I'd smile politely and tell her she looked nice in whatever it was she was wearing.

"Man alive," Leah said. She took another sip of her Log-gerhead. "I can't believe you don't remember."

In my hand, the buzzer was epileptic.

Maybe I could replace every memory I had of her with this one, right now: Leah Wyland at The Grizzly Bar, in a waterpark resort, in November, with some boyfriend, on her third overpriced vodka slushy, avoiding her kids and her boyfriend's kids. And her boyfriend. Going out of her way to make sure I remembered how she'd ruined my first relationship. Interested to know if, after all this time, she could get under my skin.

I stood from the bar stool, catching the attention of the two men at the other end of the bar. One of them gave me a smile, which I returned.

"Remember what?" I said. I pushed my stool in with a satisfying scrape across the tiled floor and walked away before she had a chance to reply.

CUSPING

July 1996

Lauren and I were born so late in Gemini season—me on the 20th and her on the 21st—we were cusping on Cancer. But I liked being a Gemini, knowing my best friend was one, too. I would rather be a twin than a bull or a scorpion. Or a Libra, which is just a set of scales trying to balance itself out. Even though we didn't look similar, sometimes I told people Lauren and I were sisters.

We hung out every day the summer we turned fifteen. Lauren's parents were fighting nonstop. Lauren would recount what her mom had said, what her dad had said, what her mom had said. Their fights were a badminton game, their angry words the shuttlecock, Lauren the only spectator in the crowd.

If we couldn't hang out, we talked on the phone. Most afternoons, when I wasn't babysitting for the Fosters down the street and Lauren wasn't helping at Vacation Bible School, were spent like this: me lying flat on my back in bed, the phone pressed hotly to my face, the sound of Lauren's voice in my ear. I called her often from the Fosters' place after I put Graham down for his nap, and sometimes when he seemed entertained enough by his blocks. I lied to the

Fosters and to my parents about how often I called Lauren. I couldn't help it. I'd see a telephone and my fingers would begin to pantomime her number.

The day it started, Lauren's dad took us to the new planetarium at the public museum. At first, I'd pushed for the mall: I wanted a frozen coffee and to walk around with Lauren, maybe hit the bookstore. But it was her father's call. He wanted to spend time with her, even though he'd acquiesced to bring me along. She told me that at the planetarium, we could look for the Gemini constellation: our own special arrangement of stars.

That's when I'd said *sure*.

The show didn't start until two p.m., so we had some time to kill. Lauren's dad had already taken us to lunch, and I sensed he'd used all his good talking points as we ate our Big Macs.

Taken alongside Lauren's mother, I didn't mind Mr. Greely all that much. But without Mrs. Greely, he was a bit of a misfit toy: a stiff, nervous guy whose smile only took root at the corners of his mouth.

At the museum, Mr. Greely made the three of us take our time through the hall of fossils. We stopped often as we shuffled along to admire the pockmarked rocks on display under thick squares of glass, each rock older than the last.

I kept trying to get Lauren out of his earshot so she could tell me what was *really* going on the way she did on the phone when we talked for so long, I had to switch ears.

To make her laugh, to distract her, to change the subject, I said out of nowhere, "That guy in the black pants? He's going to die falling down an elevator shaft chasing a butterfly."

I watched her face for a reaction. When Lauren burst open with laughter, I felt a curtain of relief wash over me.

"That woman over there," Lauren whispered, pointing to a woman in a white dress with a toddler holding her hand.

"One day her husband finds out she spent all his money on jigsaw puzzles, and he's so mad, he poisons her dinner!"

I laughed harder and louder than I needed to. But I needed Lauren to hear me laugh. I needed to hear her laugh, too. I needed to be the one to make her laugh.

"That woman," I whispered between giggles, "gets run over by a racehorse at the Kentucky Derby! The horse even runs over her hat!"

I thought that was funny because the woman had sort of a horsey face: long in the nose, not very attractive. And she *was* wearing a hat—not the oversized Derby-style hat of my fantasy, but a hat nonetheless.

"That man," Lauren snorted, "drowns in the tub! While taking a bubble bath. And listening to Enya."

The Enya detail pushed me over the edge. So clearly could I picture the man with straggly brown hair crying into a glass of wine over lost love. It felt so good to be so mean to people who were none the wiser. I laughed until I couldn't breathe, trying my best to cover my mouth with my hands.

"That woman," I countered, "buys a lottery ticket but then gives herself a paper cut with it and bleeds to death driving home. She wins a million and never sees a dime."

Lauren doubled over, grabbing my shoulder to prevent herself from falling all the way down. I thought for a second she might pee her pants like she did when we were in fourth grade on the trampoline.

If the strangers around us heard our whispers, they would never have been able to guess we were fortune-telling their demises. Who would suspect the two teen girls trailing behind Lauren's humorless father could be the imaginators of such terrible prophesies?

The more we did, the meaner they got.

That man chokes on a Twinkie.

That woman gets shot in the head with a slingshot—her kid gets her right on the temple.

I said that one because the kid orbiting the woman seemed obnoxious.

That woman falls off her roof and breaks all the bones in her body. Every. Single. One.

Our laughter echoed through the brick-lined halls of the museum. If Mr. Greely overheard what we were whispering about as he led on determinedly past the exhibit on fish species invasive to the Great Lakes, he gave no indication. We played until the lights dimmed inside the Roger B. Chaffee Planetarium and Mr. Greely shushed us and ushered us into our seats right as the star show opened.

LAUREN SPENT THE NIGHT at my house a lot that July, sleeping on the floor of my bedroom in her polka-dot sleeping bag. Mom worried it was uncomfortable—the floor of my room, even with the thick carpet—so she laid a sleeping bag under Lauren's sleeping bag for added softness. Sleepovers were usually only for weekends, but since it was summer, and since my parents knew the Greelys were having problems, they let Lauren stay over whenever she wanted. My dad even joked about making her a spare key.

We'd stay up late, quietly watching television in the den, carefully painting our nails on the coffee table. Every actor or actress on the television was subjected to our game.

Brad Pitt, with his rugged face—he was going to go skydiving and his parachute wasn't going to open. I was allowed to watch *Legends of the Fall* even though it was rated R; my mom didn't think the sex scenes were too bad. Or we would watch *Far and Away*, but that was my second choice because it was kind of boring.

Tom Cruise was going to get decapitated by an elevator when it breaks down and he's stuck between floors. The door opens and he pokes his head out to call for help, and the elevator slices his melon off like a guillotine.

Nicole Kidman, who got to kiss Tom Cruise in that movie—she was going to ski into a tree. But the collision wasn't what was going to kill her. It would be the avalanche of snow falling from the branches that would do her in.

This made Lauren scrunch her nose. "You're *so* twisted."

I grinned. Then I told her to go back to talking about what she was talking about before we started the boring movie, and she took a big sip of the root beer my dad said she could have. Her dad had been sleeping in the spare room for weeks. He'd moved his clothes in there, too.

I kept spending as much time with Lauren as possible. I ignored other friends' invitations to go to the movies. I skipped Maddie's birthday party at the roller arena—not on purpose, but the Saturday it happened was the night Lauren's parents sat her down and told her they were officially done working on the marriage. Her mom was not backing down. Her dad was moving out. There was nothing he could say, and nothing anyone could do to fix it.

Without a second thought about the party or the book I'd picked up for Maddie earlier that week, wrapped in white paper that said *Happy Birthday!* in five languages, I rode my ten-speed to Lauren's, and then she and I rode to the middle school where we sat on the bleachers for hours. Lauren cried, and I sat next to her, and I only played the Death Game once with a woman who was walking on the track holding small purple hand weights.

I made a joke about how a plane was going to land on this lady while she was exercising in the middle of an open field. Lauren stopped crying and laughed lightly. She told me I was crazy, but then she said she was lucky to have a friend like me.

"We're twins," I said. "You and me."

"Mmm."

"WHAT ABOUT MRS. PARDEE?" I asked Lauren of our home-room teacher. School started next week, and Lauren and I were lucky our class schedules aligned so well.

"I don't know," Lauren said. "I think she might die when she tries to run the Iditarod."

I laughed into the phone. "Why would anyone do that?"

I knew Lauren so well, I could imagine her shrug. "I'm sure there's a prize."

"You mean she runs the race with a team of dogs, right? She doesn't literally run the race herself."

Lauren giggled. "Yeah! Sled dogs! Like a dozen of them. Huskies. Or Alaskan Malamutes. My cousin Travis has one of those."

"Those are really pretty dogs."

"He tried to teach his how to hunt once. Didn't go so well." It was great to hear her laugh.

"So you think she freezes to death?" I asked. Mrs. Pardee was a slim woman. She'd freeze quickly, maybe.

Lauren considered. "Or, like, she doesn't pack enough food and the dogs eat her."

"Ew," I said, even though I was delighted. "Not much meat on those bones. She'd probably taste like a stick of celery," I added. I wanted Lauren to laugh again, and I wanted to think of the funniest thing Mrs. Pardee's wiry body might taste like.

"Ew," Lauren echoed. "Well anyway, I hope she lets us pick seats."

"Tracy says she doesn't." I switched the phone to my other ear and repositioned my feet on the wall. We'd been talking for half an hour, and I'd been working up the courage to get to the thing I wanted to know. I read her the Gemini horoscope from the newspaper and after we talked about its prediction, I asked, "Your dad's really moving out this weekend?"

"Yeah. He started paying rent the first of August. He's already got boxes there. But he said he needs help with the bigger stuff."

"What's the bigger stuff?"

"The bed from the spare bedroom. His desk. I don't know what else."

I nodded, and then said *mmm*, since Lauren couldn't see me over the phone. "Where's his new apartment?"

"On Fulton. He says there's a pool."

"That'll be fun." I wasn't sure what to say, but I thought I sounded upbeat.

"Maybe for a few more weeks, but soon it'll be too cold."

"Oh. It's an *outdoor* pool?"

"Duh," she said. I shouldn't have mentioned her dad moving out. But she'd brought it up last week when we'd gone out for soft-serve, and she'd cried quietly in the backseat of my sister Tracy's car as she drove us home. For her part, Tracy had pretended not to notice.

"Thought maybe it was an indoor pool."

"Hey, I gotta go. Talk to you later."

But I heard the dial tone on Lauren's end before I could say goodbye.

AFTER SCHOOL STARTED, I played the Death Game by myself a lot. It made the days pass faster, but without Lauren as an audience, it wasn't as good.

At school, I would choose a seat in the back of the class whenever I could. I'd stare at the back of everyone's heads as though I could divine their fates from their hair follicles.

Cecily was going to become a Trapeze artist and fall from the highest wire. That fit. She was a gymnast.

Morgan was going to get bitten by a spider and not even notice until the growth overtook her whole face, and a million spider babies came spilling out and into her mouth and down her throat to make her choke. I'd read that in a book somewhere.

Sometimes, I'd write predictions down in my notebook, although I was careful to start at the back, far from the practice homework sets. My worst nightmare would have entailed my math teacher catching sight of a list of twenty-nine of his pupils and how they were going to die.

Once, I asked Lauren if she ever wrote any of hers down. She'd scrunched her nose and looked at me like I was bananas, and I hadn't been able to shake that expression for days. That look of hers had begged the question, *why on Earth would I do that?*

I got paranoid someone would find my list. I began replacing names with initials, and I started drawing icons to remind myself of my idea. I would write "H.P." and I'd draw a tractor with furiously spinning blades. If someone were to see my list written that way, they'd just think I was a weird doodler. I wasn't much of an artist, although I did like to draw constellations. Our constellation. The twins outlined in bright, shining stars, holding hands in the sky.

Once, I showed Lauren one of my Gemini sketches, but she didn't know what it was. It hurt that she didn't remember it from the star show at the planetarium. But I reminded myself she was going through a hard time, and I kept capturing Death Game predictions because it was my mission to be the reason Lauren smiled at least one time a day. Sometimes at lunch I would take out my notebook and recount a few, but often there were too many people at our table, and everyone seemed annoyed when I cupped Lauren's ears with my palms and whispered into them.

Maddie even asked if we had crushes on each other, we were whispering so much. It was a joke, but Lauren told me on the phone that night that we should probably cool it—at least while at school.

In a way it was a bit of a relief: I could keep writing them down and saving them up, like a squirrel storing nuts for winter. But in another way, it made me feel strange about the game we had created together—that maybe she thought there was something wrong with it, something odd about it, and by extension, something wrong or odd about me. Inside my head, I had arguments with Lauren about the Death Game that never happened in real life. I tossed heated justifications and accusations about how she was just as much a part of the Death Game as I was, that it was just as much her brainchild as it had been mine. I wanted to tell her that she used to find it even funnier than I did. I wanted to ask her why she didn't find it as funny anymore.

I didn't tell Lauren, but more than once I had created ideas for how my own parents were going to die, how my sister was going to die.

And although I didn't tell Lauren, more than once, I had at times thought of, but never wrote down and certainly never shared with her, ideas for how she might die, too.

BY THE TIME OCTOBER rolled around, I was playing the Death Game constantly. I couldn't stop. I didn't see faces anymore; I saw knives sticking out of skulls. I saw corpses hanging from gallows. When teachers called on me, I would picture their arms and legs dismembered. I pictured their hands with no fingers when they pointed to something on the blackboard.

Whoever we were learning about in class, I became preoccupied with how they died. If a historical figure died in an interesting way, I'd lock it into my memory, use it later for the lunch lady who handed me a greasy piece of pepperoni pizza on a droopy cardboard plate.

Alexander of Greece got attacked by his pet monkey, which bit him and led to a deadly infection.

Attila the Hun, despite being an incredible warrior, was said to have died of a severe nosebleed.

Adolf Frederick, the King of Sweden, ate himself to death—so it was said.

It was satisfying to read about fascinating and fantastical ways to die.

I thought about the assistant principal getting attacked by a monkey—one with colorful patches on his body. I pictured my art teacher, whom I had always liked, surrounded in a room with towers of sheet cakes and cheese pizzas and two liters of soda.

In gym, Cam got hit in the face with a stray red volleyball, and when he was sent to the bathroom to take care of his nosebleed, I imagined the janitor finding the corpse later, after everyone had gone home for the day.

I didn't share these with Lauren often anymore. Maybe just once a week. When I did, she would mostly change the subject.

I *did* share that we should dress as twins for Halloween—the Gemini girls. I would wear a wig. I'd already bought one that I thought matched her hair pretty well. We could both wear our acid-wash jeans and black hoodies, and our red Skechers. We could do our makeup the same way. Every day that passed where she didn't make plans to go trick-or-treating with me increased the tight feeling in my chest that she was never going to.

I also kept asking to see her dad's apartment, which was small with only one bathroom, but did have a second bedroom for her. She stayed with him Monday through Wednesday, and every other weekend. I asked Lauren if it was hard to live out of a duffel bag. She'd frowned the way she had at my assertion that her crush Jonathan might die in a plane expedition to the Bermuda Triangle as his crew tried to uncover the unsolved mystery of the disappearance of Amelia Earhart. She hadn't found that funny.

I'd also tried not to read anything into the fact that it had taken her three whole weeks to give me the number of the landline that rang at her dad's apartment, which she said he was taking his time to set up, and it wasn't as easy as all that, and she was going through something I wasn't going through, and even though she knew I thought I understood, my parents were still in love and my family was still perfect, and could I give her some space?

SO I DID. I stopped calling for a few days. My fingers ached with the old itch to dial her number. It was awful, made worse when my dad asked Friday at dinner why my twin wasn't spending the night; he'd stocked the fridge with Mug for her. I stared at the Fosters' phone Saturday night as I babysat Graham. I'd given Lauren their number in case I was babysitting and she needed to talk. It was foolish to think she'd call me there that night, since she didn't even know that's where I was, but I held out that hope till I heard the Fosters' car pull in their driveway just after ten o'clock anyway.

I didn't hear from Lauren at all for five days. I didn't see her for five days. She wasn't in school—at least I was pretty sure. At first, I thought maybe she was skipping Mrs. Pardee's class to avoid me, going off campus for lunch to avoid me, but Maddie said she hadn't seen her, either. Finally, I broke down and called her house on Tuesday, but no one was home. I called her dad's line that night, too, but the phone just rang and rang.

Wednesday, I was doodling stars in a line while the principal rattled on with his daily announcements on the loudspeaker when I saw Lauren walk in. If I were going to die right then, it would have been of a heart attack. I could picture my own heart exploding in my chest like a bomb in the silence between us as she settled into her seat.

"Hey," I said.

Lauren had already opened a novel, but she wasn't looking at its dark pages. Her blonde hair was hanging down as a curtain around her face.

"Hey," I said, louder this time. "Are you mad at me, or something?"

It wasn't that she wasn't interested in playing the Death Game anymore. It wasn't that she'd asked for space and ignored me for five days, or that she hadn't returned my calls at all, or that she obviously didn't like my Halloween idea. It was all of it together. It was the fact that my notebook was overrun with different ways to die, and it didn't feel as funny as it did before, and that felt like her fault. I'd worked so hard to craft laughter into every humid day that summer. I'd worked endlessly to let her know I was there for her, that I was her twin, and somehow, none of that mattered to her at all.

She turned her face toward me, and I could see her bottom lip was quivering. Twin red blotches bloomed on her cheeks, and I knew this meant she was working hard not to cry. "I want you to stay away from me," she hissed. "You caused this. You and your stupid game. You're a freak and I want you to stay away from me."

I blinked. I was sure I'd misheard somehow. She'd asked for space, and I'd left her alone. For nearly a week. I felt a bit like a fish with his lips on a hook, and I was opening my mouth to argue when I noticed Cecily had stood from her desk and was giving Lauren a hug. Which Lauren was returning. Mrs. Pardee looked up, but then I saw Mrs. Pardee give Cecily a little smile and the smallest possible nod.

"I'm so sorry for your loss," I heard Cecily say to Lauren.

"What—what loss?" I whispered to Lauren. "What's going on?"

She didn't answer, so I whispered it again. Cecily leveled me with her eyes, and I tried to listen, even as in my mind, I was picturing her falling from a fire-lit hoop high in the air.

"Her cousin Travis died. Where have you been?"

Cecily let go of Lauren and sat back down at her desk, and I sat dumbfounded for a second as Mr. Hammond on the PA system rattled on about the upcoming fundraiser.

I just stared at the tent of Lauren's hair, waiting for her to turn to me so I could say something else, but she never did. The entire homeroom period passed. Lauren never looked my way, and when the bell rang she was up like a shot and out the door.

Walking out of the classroom, I tapped Cecily on the shoulder, and I didn't care that I sounded like I was about to cry, too.

"What happened to Travis? Will you tell me, please? She won't talk to me, for some reason." I pretended there was nothing the matter between Lauren and me. I remembered meeting Travis once, at one of Lauren's family reunions. Her dad's side. He had a nice smile. He'd offered me a soda.

Cecily rolled her eyes. She sighed dramatically and moved out of the way of the flow of traffic. "He was hunting Saturday, up north. Deer. With Lauren's uncles. There was an accident. He got shot. He didn't make it. That's all I know."

"Oh my God," was all I could say. "I had no idea." My eyes welled up with tears, which finally seemed to make Cecily soften.

She started to walk again, looking back at me to make sure I was following. "Yeah. She didn't, like, really tell anyone. She found out Saturday, and just, you know, took a few days off school. Maddie heard it through Mrs. Dalinger. Anyway, I think the memorial is this week, but then the funeral isn't till this weekend. I forget. But anyway, Lauren didn't want to just, like, keep missing school."

"Oh my God," I said again. I was crushed for two reasons: that this had happened, and that I hadn't been there for Lauren. And then a third reason knocked the wind out of me: Lauren hadn't wanted me to be.

Cecily and I had reached the hallway with her locker. I watched her put in the combination and pull the metal door open with a squeak. Part of me knew I also needed to get my stuff from my own locker and head to Social Studies, but I felt glued to Cecily and her words as way off in the distance, right at the end of the hallway, I caught the last sight of Lauren's blonde hair whipping around the corner.

"Yeah," Cecily said, sighing. "It's sad. He was *so* young. And what a terrible way to die."

"Yeah," I said. "It is. That's horrible. I'm sorry. Tell Lauren I'm sorry."

BABY REGISTRY

Miriam and Jamie

Miriam holds up a box depicting a red-haired woman typing with both hands on a laptop. Overtop her clothes, on each breast, a breast pump hangs. The woman is smiling.

"Is that what's it like?" Miriam asks.

I laugh. "One hundred percent no."

Miriam frowns and sticks the breast pump box back on the Target shelf. "It can't be that comfortable. Is it comfortable?"

I shake my head.

She says, "No one has ever been happier to be writing an email than this woman."

I laugh lightly and put the baby carrier I'd been holding back on its peg. "I've never tried the hands-free thing, but then again, I've never had an email that couldn't wait. Maybe she's the President. You don't know she's not."

Miriam looks at me for a long moment and I wonder, as I sometimes do, if I've taken the wrong tack—that she was deeply wanting me to say something else entirely, maybe something to bring her reassurance and comfort, but I've blown it by trying to be funny. I've reached instead for something Miriam would say, if Miriam were me. The byproduct of spending so many years with someone, maybe; did they still love you for what uniquely makes you *you*, what you bring to the table? Or is it only to be expected the two of us by now were melted into versions of the same person?

Aside from Miriam being half a foot shorter than me and six months pregnant, we appear as alternate versions of each other. That, and Miriam looks tired. Which is to be expected, of course; by six months pregnant with Ethan, I had little energy to do much but lounge on the couch. There'd been something so sinfully and wonderfully indulgent about those last few weeks. I let myself be lazy. Other than being tired, I loved being pregnant. I loved it when strangers smiled at me in the grocery store as I pushed a cart ahead of my bulging belly. One woman even stopped me near the checkout at D&W—a kind-looking, older woman in a beige coat. She'd put a hand on my forearm, looked at me with her clear blue eyes, and told me I looked so beautiful.

But today is not about me. I'm doing my best not to make it about me. To keep mum about what I remember about being pregnant and having Ethan, which was a few years ago.

I don't have the vocabulary to articulate to my best friend the ways in which time altogether is about to change for her—that whole days and entire weeks will meld now, and she will find herself an alien on a new planet, inhabiting a place in the universe entirely different than the one she occupies now.

Which is Target on the east side of town, eleven a.m. on a Sunday. I am taking her to lunch after this. We'll fight the after-church crowd. I'm hoping she doesn't bow out. Next door is a Panera, and I'm craving a bread bowl.

"Well, I'm registering for this double-boob pumper for shits and giggles," Miriam says, flipping the package over to locate its barcode on the back. She points her smartphone at it and waits for the online baby registry to accept the new addition. "It'll be like a litmus test to see which of my friends is demented enough to buy me a medieval torture device."

"Your sister, to get back at you," I joke, but Miriam doesn't laugh. I kick myself again. I take a sip of the coffee we treated ourselves to from the store's Starbucks kiosk and make a mental note to stop trying to be funny—to stop trying to do an impression of Miriam. She needs me to be *me* today, I think—the friend who's already done this.

"It's my *mom* who wants to get back at me," Miriam says. "You know… unwed mother… Rich and me having a bastard."

This time I get it right. I don't try to be funny. I give her a look that I know she knows means I understand.

A long moment passes. Miriam says, "What else do I need?"

I lick the froth off my lips and frown, considering. "You've got sheets and bedding, diapers and wipes…You'll probably want to register for some more little things that people *like* to buy—like onesies and bath toys. But I recommend not registering for a lot of clothes or like, blankets. Babies always get ten million blankets. You'll be swimming in them."

Miriam nods and we walk sort of together to the next aisle. I'm not wrong; she is tired. She isn't accustomed to not being the one with the plan. I'm not accustomed to telling her what to do, even though she's begged me to come with her and make this registry. Her sister Annabelle and their mother had been pestering Miriam to make it since they sent out invitations for her baby shower that included the line *Miriam and Rich are registered at Target,* even though she wasn't. This evidently had annoyed Annabelle and Miriam's mother, who had to field the RSVPs and stomach complaints about how attendees had gone online to look for the registry, but there was nothing there. A slew of texts had ensued to me from Miriam—screenshots of text message exchanges she'd had with Annabelle, who conveyed her annoyance with Miriam. *They have online guides,* Annabelle had texted, a little pointedly. *It's so easy. Just make one!*

I pick up a mesh bag of bath toys—soft, rubbery-silicone zoo animals, maybe a dozen, all with friendly faces. In the real world, these animals would not get along, and I pause, placing their hierarchy in my mind. Most are mammals—a lion, an elephant, a monkey, a bear. The zebra too, and he is the cutest with a stalk of green grass sticking out of his mouth like a cigar. I wonder if the menagerie has been curated on purpose. A series of animals who feed their young milk, a comfort to a young mother trying to breastfeed her own baby.

I'm holding the bag and thinking about how one of the strangest things about being a pregnant woman was confronting my own *mammality*—if that's a word. *Mammal-ness.* The fact that I am a mammal, too. That it had been easy to ignore my breasts that were previously just there for aesthetics and pleasure until they were there for necessity. I was a mammal just like that smiley-faced tiger, and I guarded Ethan just like any other mama cat in the wild.

"Register for these," I tell Miriam. Obediently, she hovers her phone over the barcode and a satisfying beep lets her know that the item has been successfully added. "People love to buy stuff like this."

She nods, and I don't mention that one thing she is going to need to watch out for is that they don't accumulate water and get moldy inside, as I learned once when I was squirting water out of a rubber duck. I'd almost gagged. Suddenly I regret encouraging her to register for bath toys that might get skunky without her notice.

I don't know how to prepare Miriam for all the things she is going to have to worry about. I don't know how to prepare Miriam at all for what's about to happen to her and the ways in which her life is going to change, so I smile and point at the baby baths and make too much fuss over the one Mike and I used for Ethan.

And then for some reason, an old memory flies into my mind as I watch Miriam read the back of the box and crack a lewd joke about babies peeing in the tub.

The night of my bachelorette party, before Mike and I got married, Miriam had taken me to a bar. A few bars. She'd made me wear a tiara and pink sash that said BACHELOR-ETTE in bright bold letters.

We were dancing, and I'd lost track of how many drinks I'd had but not the fact that I was having a wonderful time when Miriam clocked two men, standing nearby, who'd been staring. I thought they were mostly looking at Miriam.

One man was tall with brown hair swept across his fore-head. He had a movie star quality I could tell Miriam was going to be talking about tomorrow. He said something in her ear, but Miriam was just pointing at me, I'd guess telling this man I was going to be married next week, and wasn't that a shame? The man waved at me and gave me a thumbs-up, but his expression didn't match the gesture. Even drunk, I knew he believed getting married so young was a stupid endeavor.

Suddenly, though, I felt a man close in on my dance space, and I realized it was his friend. This man was shorter with black hair growing a little gray at the edges. He had a kind smile. He was wearing a maroon polo shirt, and when he got closer, I noticed the fabric had darker horizontal stripes. For some reason, he and the tall man didn't seem like a likely pair at all. They didn't match the way Miriam and I did—a pair of salt and pepper shakers, my mom once said.

"You're getting married, huh," the man said to me, loudly.

I grinned and pointed at the BACHELORETTE sash on my chest. "You're quick."

He laughed and took a drink from the beer in his hand. "Congratulations," he said. "I'd buy you a drink, but you seem okay."

"I'm great," I said. He laughed. He had nice olive skin. He wasn't exactly dancing, but then again, neither was I. Miriam and his tall friend, however, had quickly closed the distance between them, and a few of the other friends in our bachelorette party were whispering in each other's ears, hands covering their mouths to hide what they were saying. I could guess.

"You *are* great," he said. "I wish you all the best. Orhan, by the way," he said, and I realized that he was giving me his name.

"Oh," I said, and instead of offering my own, I blurted out, "I love that author! Orhan Pamuk!"

He smiled and seemed to brighten. "Yeah. What's your favorite of his?"

We'd stopped even trying to dance, which was a bit of a relief to me. The music had changed to something with more of an R&B feel. I said, "Definitely *Snow*."

"Yeah." Orhan got a weird smile on his face. "That's my wife's favorite, too."

"Oh yeah? She sounds smart."

"She is," he said, looking serious. "She's my best friend."

"Oh, that's great. That's nice."

"It's really important that you marry your best friend, you know."

"Yeah," I said. I wasn't quite sure what to say.

We stood there for a second, and I took another drink. The weird thing about being the BACHELORETTE was being on the receiving end of so much attention. This was a role better suited for Miriam, but she and Rich were on another break.

"Are *you* marrying your best friend?" Orhan asked. I realized I hadn't given him my name, but he didn't seem to mind.

"Of course," I said.

"What's his name—the guy you're marrying?" I brush past the fact that it's weird Orhan doesn't want my name but rather, for some reason, my fiancé's. To him, I guess I'm just BACHELORETTE. Nameless girl at a loud bar. Friend of the girl his friend is hitting on.

"Mike," I said.

He gave me a goofy look. "And you're sure about that?" I nodded. "Yup." But in that moment, the way Orhan was looking at me, the confidence with which he asserted his wife loved *Snow*, made me look down at my left hand. It was a big diamond—a princess cut solitaire. Bigger than I imagined Mike could afford, but there it was, on my left hand for months, like it had business being there. A quick romance. A quick engagement. No pregnancy, just an urgency Mike had expressed at not wanting to wait a minute longer than necessary to start life with me.

"How long have you and Mike been together?" Orhan asked me.

"Like a year," I answered. I almost added, *I'm Jamie, by the way*, but I took another drink instead. There was at least one more bar Miriam had suggested we go to, but I wondered if meeting Tall Guy was going to change that plan. His lips were close to her neck as he was saying something in her ear, and she had her hand resting on his shoulder, holding her white wine spritzer precariously.

"Less than a year?" Orhan asked.

"Yup," I said, even though it was clear he'd misheard me. Mike and I had been together thirteen months, actually, but there didn't seem to be much point arguing with a stranger.

"Okay, but I'm telling you, marry your best friend," Orhan said. "In the end, it's all that matters. The romance and the sex and all that—trust me—it fades. Like *really* fast."

"Huh," I said. And of course, I didn't believe him.

"Trust me. You're doomed if you don't."

"I'm so over this," Miriam says as we reach the aisle with pacifiers. I snap back to the present as she adds, "This is a particular kind of tedium."

I nod. I don't know why I've thought about Orhan and that night. It was so long ago. *That night was about me. Today is about my best friend*, I chide myself. I need to be more supportive. We need to wrap this up and get lunch and talk about other things for a while.

"Pacifiers are hard," I say. "Honestly, the baby won't even know what she wants. You'll wind up trying a few. I'll look and see if I saved any," I offer, "but you could always register for a few brands. Some people might want, like, a cheaper add-on item."

"Beam me up," Miriam says, grabbing a few packages at random and scanning them to her registry.

She picks up a tube of Vaseline and looks at me. "Another good add-on?"

"Hold off," I say. "There's a product out there called Bag Balm. You'll want it for, like, everything."

"*Bag Balm?*" she asks.

"It sounds absurd, I know—I'll get you some. It's *like* Vaseline, but better. Mike's dad used it on the cows."

"*What?*" Miriam says, and her eyes light up. "So now I am fully a milk-producing animal?"

"I mean, not for forever."

"It sounds horrifying," she says—and I know she's talking about Bag Balm, but I understand she's also talking about all of this. The whole shebang—the belly, the birth, the nursing. The whole thing where a baby was going to come out of her body and for years, she was destined to do nothing but worry over its every sneeze, its every move—the way I still worry over Ethan. He's three, and I thought my anxiety would slow by now, but it shows no sign of letting up. I will worry about him every second of my life. I don't tell my best friend what that's like.

"It's this miracle product that heals everything. You'll want to get some. Trust me. You're doomed if you don't," I say.

This makes Miriam giggle. It was a weird thing for me to say, but she doesn't say that. "I'm *doomed* if I don't?"

I shake my head, scoffing. Maybe she thinks I was just trying to be funny. "Sorry," I say. "I think I'm just hungry. I think you've got a good enough registry. Your mom and Annabelle will be happy. Let's get out of here. Let me buy you lunch."

STAG'S

When I told Ashley I didn't mind nannying Hayden because baby pee smells like buttered popcorn, I was certain I'd just taken our new friendship, forged in the boredom of Psych 200, off the rails. It was my first semester, and I was desperate to make friends. My last report card at Northern Michigan sent me packing, tail between my legs, taking up residence in my childhood bedroom, enrolling in CC, and nannying on the side.

But on Thursday, after class, Ashley turned to me and asked me to hang out.

"I want to go to this bar in Big Rapids Saturday."

"Sure. Uh… one problem. I'm not twenty-one."

"Your birthday was last week," she said, frowning. She swept her bangs out of her eyes and pressed her lips together like she was putting on lipstick.

"I just turned twenty."

"You're *twenty*?"

"Yup."

"Huh." The class we shared was required for almost all academic programs, so it was full of people who sort of cared about psychology, but also, didn't. When I wasn't in class, I nannied for Hayden. When I wasn't nannying for Hayden, I was at home. Because that's what all cool part-time college students who live at home—who also recently got dumped by their boyfriends in the parking lot of the mall—do.

"You know what? I think it'll be fine. The last time I went, they didn't card."

"Okay," I said, grinning. Ashley made Psych 200 palatable. She was fun. We shared notes and swapped glances whenever our instructor was being weird.

Not unlike myself.

What kind of weirdo talks about baby urine? Even if it does smell like buttered popcorn?

A weirdo like me.

Who now had plans Saturday night.

With maybe a new friend.

ASHLEY PICKED ME UP in her Camry Saturday night, which smelled like cigarettes and air freshener. In the passenger side, I pulled the seatbelt over my jacket, hoping it was the right kind of cool. She appraised me for a moment before telling me I looked cute.

"Thanks," I said. "You too."

And she did. She was wearing a black mini skirt with gray suede boots, a white tank top under a thin teal cardigan. Also, way more eye makeup than I was used to seeing on her on Tuesdays and Thursdays from two fifteen to four o'clock p.m.

I'd told my folks I was going out with a friend from class, and my mom had been excited. My dad had given me his standard look. I was too old to have a curfew, but also beholden to my parental landlords. Maybe next semester I could move out. Get an apartment. I was saving a lot, considering I spent so little. Maybe I could afford an apartment with a roommate.

We made small talk until we hit the highway, and I realized she'd let my question hang in the air.

"Wait—so what bar are we going to?"

Ashley looked over at me, one hand on the steering wheel, a grin on her face. "Stag's."

"*Stag's*? God, that sounds like a terrible bar."

"Oh, it is," she said, laughing. "Total dive."

"Why are we going there?"

Ashley glanced in her mirror before changing lanes. She was picking up speed as we got away from the city. It would be dark soon. I realized I didn't know her last name.

"To see a band."

Sort of. Piece by piece, I pulled it out of Ashley. We were driving almost an hour to Stag's to see a guy she had a crush on. A guy she worked with at the bookstore in the mall. A guy who played in a band. In short: to see Craig.

"He's the *lead singer*." She drummed her hand on the steering wheel. "He's hot. You're gonna die."

I laughed. I realized I hadn't been out much since Patrick had dumped me—ironically, in the parking lot of the same mall where Ashley worked. What a place to get dumped. We'd had lunch at the food court, gotten into a fight. I'd had a giant Diet Pepsi and really had to pee. What I couldn't get over is that we were long-distance for an entire semester and he broke up with me once I moved home. The amount of time I spent on the phone with him and traveling back and forth from Grand Rapids to Northern Michigan murdered my GPA, but he'd waited until I moved home to dump me.

"Are you going to ask him out?" I asked.

"Of course not!"

"Oh. Well, does he like you?" It seemed like the next pragmatic question.

"I think so," she said, smiling again.

"How do you know?"

"Like during my shift, he'll come over if I'm on register, and like, he totally didn't *need* to, you know? After I'm done, sometimes we hang out."

"Sounds promising."

Ashley just giggled. It seemed her crush was a fire that didn't require extra fuel from me.

"What about you?" she asked. "Anyone special right now?"

"Not since Patrick."

"Parking lot Patrick?"

"Yup," I said.

"Well!" She reached over to pat my leg, like she was giving my left knee a series of high fives. "That could change tonight. You never know."

"Are you suggesting I'll meet my soulmate at Stag's?"

She giggled again. "You never know! I feel like Craig is mine."

"Wow. That's heavy."

Ashley nodded, her lips pressed together. "Mmm."

"*SHIT*," ASHLEY SAID as she put the Camry in park.

"What?"

"They're carding."

I'd been shaking down my purse for a breath mint, not really paying attention. Following her gaze, I saw a line by the door of Stag's, which fit the image I'd drawn in my mind: log-cabin building, big neon sign. Through the windows I could see fake deer heads on the wall. I could almost feel the sticky floor under my black ballet flats. "They're *carding*?" I parroted.

"I'm sorry. I swear they didn't last time."

"I believe you."

"You wanna try anyway?"

"Try to get in?"

"Yeah," Ashley nodded. "You're really pretty. Maybe if you just tell him you won't order anything?"

My stomach dropped. I'd only ever tried to sneak into a bar once. Patrick was with his friends and they'd convinced me it was a good idea. Or that it would be funny. I don't remember.

It was neither a good idea, nor was it funny. A bouncer with full sleeve tattoos had yelled at me, and I'd wound up sitting on the curb with Patrick's friend Gabe while Patrick got wasted inside. Because *he* was twenty-one. My most recent Instagram stalk showed him at that same bar, with the same guys. I wondered if he'd remembered me crying that night.

"I don't know."

"Please? Let's just try." She ran her fingers through her hair. "I have a feeling something good is going to happen tonight."

I sighed, unclicking my seatbelt. I *did* need to make friends. Stop being such a loner who spent all her time on social media or with a boy who could only babble *mama, dada, baba,* on repeat.

"OH MY GOD," Ashley squealed, squeezing my arm as we walked through the entryway and to the big bar in the back of Stag's. "I can't believe that *worked!*"

I couldn't either. I let my eyes adjust to the dim lighting. Indeed, those were deer heads on the wall. So many deer heads. I counted eight.

"He, like, looked at your ID, and then at you, and then he just let you in! He must have thought you were cute."

"Yup," I said, studying the black ink circle stamp drying on the back of my hand.

"Let's get a drink."

"No thanks, I'm good."

"What?" Ashley shrieked. "You just got into a bar a full year before you're supposed to, and you don't even want a drink?"

"Well," I considered. "Who's driving home?"

"Me, goofball. But don't worry, I'm totally responsible."

I sighed and reached into my wallet for a five-dollar bill. "Okay, but will you order it for me? A beer. I don't care which. I don't think I can keep a straight face."

Ashley took my five and rolled her eyes. "Go find a table. Near the stage, okay? They're coming out soon."

I sat at a table and fished my phone from my purse. I thought about checking in on Facebook, just in case Patrick was following me, too. He'd be impressed I'd gotten into a bar. Then, I thought better of it. Someone would see and it would get back to my mom somehow. Or—just as likely—Patrick would see and know exactly what I was really trying to say: showing him I was out at a bar. That I was fine. That I was cool. That I was having fun without him.

And with a new friend, who started screaming the moment the band took the stage.

Their name: The Dadbods.

I realized, when the lead singer came out and greeted the crowd, which had grown to about forty people, that Craig was old. Old enough to be Ashley's dad. He looked like a dad. He had a dadbod. Because he was probably fifty. Older.

"Wait," I said, yelling over the loud guitar chords. Their first song was one I didn't know, but apparently a cover. I wanted to make sure I was reading the situation right—that half a bottle of the cheap lager Ashley had put in front of me wasn't going to my head. I didn't feel buzzed. I just had a sour taste in my mouth. "Which one is Craig?"

"That one!" Ashley said, jutting her chin toward the lead singer. "He's *the assistant manager!*"

I sat back in my chair and took a swig of beer. When a waitress had passed our table, Ashley had ordered a second mixed drink, and she was almost done with it. I realized there was a good chance I was going to be driving us home.

As The Dadbods' fourth song moved into its chorus, I studied Craig and realized he was staring at Ashley. I glanced at her. She was smiling and swaying back and forth in her chair, occasionally holding her drink in the air. She raised her hands and clapped exuberantly when the song ended.

Craig winked at her, then turned his back to the crowd to take a pull from the longneck sitting on a speaker.

"You wanna get a pitcher?" Ashley asked me, loudly. I noticed for the first time a tattoo near her shoulder, visible under her sweater. Birds on a thin branch.

"I'm good. But if you want to."

She was a little clumsy on her feet. She leaned in to whisper something in my ear. "Don't let anyone take my spot!"

The Dadbods played another song—this one I knew: a slower, sweeter version of "Brown Eyed Girl." A few people began to dance at tables around me. I realized more acutely we were among the youngest people in the bar. I also realized that The Dadbods were actually pretty good, and that if I squinted the right way, Craig was kind of cute. Just old. Receding hairline. Wrinkles around the eyes. Round glasses.

I assessed my bottle and saw I had about a third left. Then I told myself under no circumstance was I to finish it.

"God, I love this song!" Ashley said, returning to the table. The pitcher sloshed as she set it down, foamy beer spilling down its side. "Help yourself."

"Thanks." The question of how long she wanted to stay was near my lips, but the pitcher was my answer. I sat back again, cupping my Bud Light with my palm, hoping Ashley wouldn't notice how empty it was.

She didn't. She didn't seem to notice anything but Craig.

And once I noticed the gold ring on his left hand, I didn't really notice anything else about him.

During the next song, I told Ashley I needed to make a phone call outside. She didn't ask any questions, even as I asked her for the keys. Then, I sat in the driver's seat for maybe forty-five minutes, the windows rolled down. It was a nice night and my phone could access the Wi-Fi. STAGS, in all caps—that was the name. No password. Not concerned with security. I scrolled through Instagram, then Facebook, then played around applying different filters to some photos

I'd taken that week of Hayden. I had an extremely cute one of him in his crib, smiling up at me. If I were his mom, I'd post it, but it felt weird for me to post it as his nanny, so I didn't.

I looked up when I saw a pair of people walking toward Ashley's car. It was the bouncer who had carded us, supporting Ashley, who was struggling to walk.

Immediately, I could tell she was crying.

"Hey," the bouncer said. To my surprise, he sounded kind. On the exterior, he looked like a tough guy: bald, full beard, big muscles—kind of like the bouncer who had yelled at me last semester. But this guy was soft-spoken. Sweet, even.

"Hi," I said, sitting up straighter. I wasn't sure if I should open the door or not, and as I was deciding, he asked if he could put Ashley in the passenger's side.

"Sure," I said. Ashley was sobbing and saying something I couldn't understand. I felt bad I'd left her in there for so long. Had she finished that pitcher? She was a mess of smeared mascara. There was something on her sweater.

"You can get her home?" he asked, leaning his shoulder into Ashley's car. His face was lit by the car's interior lights, and I saw that his eyes were kind, too—a pretty shade of hazel. He was looking at me intently, and I could tell he cared about what was happening.

"Yeah," I said. "I'm—I'm good."

"Good. I had a good feeling about you," he said. "I can always tell about people."

"Yeah," I said. "Thanks."

He was still looking at me, and for a long moment I just held his gaze. Then he smiled at me and looked like he wanted to say something. I smiled back at him. When we'd arrived, I'd thought he was older, but staring at him now, I realized he was probably closer to twenty-five than anything.

"Thanks," he said again.

With that, he shut the passenger door of Ashley's car and turned to walk back into Stag's. At the entrance, he turned and gave me a little wave. I almost missed it because I was helping Ashley take off her sweater. She pressed her forehead to the dashboard. "What the hell just happened?" she sobbed.

The drive back felt longer. Eventually, Ashley quieted down and I was able to understand her address. I parked her car at her apartment, and her roommate helped me get her inside, get her a big glass of water.

I took an Uber home and smiled when I saw Dad had left the porch light on, like he'd been doing for years.

IT WAS TUESDAY after Psych 200 before I pulled the whole story from Ashley.

She'd gone up to Craig, between songs. She'd told Craig how she felt about him. She'd told Craig she had feelings for him.

He'd told her she was crazy. He was married. She had the wrong idea. She'd read the signs all wrong. He'd just been friendly. She was crazy, he said. She said that a few times. It stood out, considering the topic in class that week had been mental illness and the societal stigma tied to it.

"The *worst* part?" she said. We were packing our backpacks and shuffling out of the classroom. "Now he's avoiding me like the plague. It's like he's afraid of me. He sees me coming and literally runs the other way. It's *embarrassing*."

"Are you going to quit?"

She looked down. "I don't know. I want to, but I like the bookstore. Plus, it's easy money. And I feel like I'm not ready to *not* see him all the time, you know?"

"Yeah. I get it."

I didn't, though. I had no idea why she was chasing after a married man who was so much older than her, who told her she was crazy. Seemed to me like there would be nothing but pain down that road, and I had no idea why she wanted to go down it.

We didn't say anything for a moment. I thought about telling Ashley that Craig was the crazy one, that of course he should like her back. Telling her that Craig was the crazy one felt like something her best friend would do, and I wasn't sure we were going to be best friends after all. So I held my tongue. I didn't say anything else. For some reason, saying nothing felt like the right thing to do.

INTERWOVEN

He'd said it over salad—a lovely, large wedge of iceberg plated with a side of bacon, a ramekin of ranch. He wasn't wrong, and he hadn't said it to hurt my feelings.

He'd said, "A normal person would just enjoy this."

As with other habits—sticking a meat thermometer in the chicken I'd baked to see 165 degrees—Cade wasn't being mean. He wasn't being malicious. He was just right.

Whenever we fought, which wasn't often, Cade was always nice to me. We got along well by nature—even stretched thin as we were by the threadbare stress of a newborn.

So, I wasn't thinking of Cade's words in any injurious way when I woke at three forty-five a.m. in a strange bed with unfamiliar sheets, huddled next to the comfort of him. Our bed at home, I would have argued, was nicer than this hotel king, but it was our second anniversary and Cade had insisted on a night of freedom.

"Won't we be just as *free* at home," I'd argued, "and $220 richer?"

"There's *company* at home," Cade had said. "Even without Ava."

He'd been referring to Gummy, our cat. Gummy hated our baby and took his feelings out on the living room curtains first, then the couch, and recently, the upholstered chairs in the dining room. Luckily, those were Ikea-chic and not worth much. Still. Cade was as frustrated as I was that our apartment had been upended first by our newborn daughter, Ava, then by a storm of destruction rendered by a salty feline.

I'd Googled the traditional gift for a second anniversary, and the Internet had reliably supplied the answer: cotton.

"It says our relationship is *maturing*," I'd told Cade. "We're flexible, but strong. Each of our fibers is becoming interwoven with the other person's."

Cade had snort-laughed. "So let's skip gifts," he'd suggested. "Get a hotel and a nice dinner instead. Gummy would just destroy new towels. Or sheets. Or whatever else is cotton."

I'd laughed. He was right.

And frankly, a night away was doable since Ava and I had given up on breastfeeding after the third month. She was all formula now. The switch came sooner than I would have liked, but things were smoother now in the new world order.

A normal person would just enjoy this: a night out, a night off, a getaway. A nice dinner and a beautiful hotel.

A normal person would soak this in.

So why couldn't I? It was 3:52 a.m.

At dinner, after the salad, there'd been a lovely plate of fettuccine—and tiramisu Cade ordered while I was in the bathroom, even though I told him I didn't need it. We weren't dessert-ordering people; we were young and broke people. His eyes were almost shining as he split it with me, and I loved him so much for that.

What I didn't tell him was that I hadn't needed to pee when I'd gone to the bathroom. I'd only needed to check my phone without him seeing, because he'd already chided me three times: twice as we were getting ready for dinner, once after the waiter brought bread.

"Will you *stop*?" he'd asked me. "Everything's fine. More wine?"

A normal person would enjoy this.

"Sure," I'd said.

"She's *fine*," Cade had said.

"Who?" I'd said.

He could have been referring to Ava or his mother, Caroline, who was watching Ava overnight. Away from us for the first night ever. She was so little. I wondered if Caroline would make her bottles the same way Cade and I did, crouching down to make sure the right amount of room temperature water was in the bottle before adding the formula. I wondered if Caroline would level off the formula in the handy plastic scoop that came with the container or with the back edge of a clean butter knife.

"They're. *Both*. Fine," he'd said, punching each word. But he was smiling. He'd leaned over the table to kiss me on the temple. "Besides, don't you have my mom's ringtone as something special?"

I had to smile then. Embarrassing, but true. I loved to pick different ringtones for everyone in my contacts list—at least my close friends and family. It had been fun to give Cade's mom the Neil Diamond song a few weeks before our wedding. Two years ago now. So much had happened already. Ava had happened already. We hadn't exactly been trying for a baby, but we hadn't been doing much to prevent a baby, either, and now here we were. Interwoven. The fabric of our identities growing ever more together.

"Yes," I said. "She's 'Sweet Caroline.'"

"So you'll know if she calls," he said. "And she'd only call if something were terribly wrong. Right? She's under strict instruction to *only* call if something's wrong with Ava."

"Right," I said.

"So you can *relax*," Cade said. Then he'd topped off my glass.

In these small ways, Cade was the opposite of Zach Blanchard, the dark-haired guy who had been my boyfriend right before Cade. Zach was the I-told-you-so kind. He loved having a front-row seat to my mistakes: confusing words like *conscience* and *conscious*, struggling to download the right parking app.

More than once, I'd wondered if dating Cade directly after Zach had sped our love along like a mudslide. If more time had passed between the two of them—more than a fortnight—maybe I'd have been less tempted to compare them.

But Cade was great. What started as a rebound grew deep roots. I made no attempt to slow our engagement, nor the small wedding that followed seven months later. I loved the way Cade made Zach disappear in the rear-view mirror.

We were stuffed leaving Florentina's. I leaned on Cade's arm, luxuriated in the feel of his long body stretched next to mine. I loved curling my frame into his, tucking my angles and rounded edges into the places of his body where they fit.

I was glad he knew where our hotel was. In my mind, a vague map of downtown was sketched, but it was as though a toddler had drawn it. Among the tall buildings and same-looking parking structures—and with all the wine—I felt a little dizzy and lost. Not in an altogether bad way. I couldn't remember the last time I'd had this much to drink.

In the hotel elevator, after the doors closed, I reached into my sequined clutch. A far cry from a diaper bag. It was so small, it held only my phone, my ID (in case I couldn't pass at dinner), one credit card, and one lipstick. I opened the clutch and made like I was searching for the lipstick, but really, I was making a clumsy grope at my phone, disturbing it awake. I thought the move was sly, but Cade had clocked it.

"Stop it. I'm begging you." Cade grabbed my waist gently with both hands. His fingers near my rib cage made me blush. This was an old trick. I was pleased it still worked.

Like the dessert, the hotel room was another extravagance. Cade took off his coat and came back to me immediately to unzip the back of my dress. I wasn't cold, but there were goosebumps on my arms just the same from the sudden feel of air on my skin, from the dress falling off my body, from Cade's fingers unhooking my bra. He turned me around and gently pushed me onto the bed. As was instinctive, I looked for Gummy. Her favorite thing to do was camouflage herself among throw pillows—especially on Cade's side, and especially lately, as Ava's loud crying made her nervous, and our bed was the quietest oasis in our small apartment.

Cade grinned his most devilish grin, pulled down my most tummy-concealing shapewear. "Just enjoy this," he said.

3:58 A.M.

Maybe the wine had worn off. Red wine seemed to like to wake me up in a wave of anxiety. It hadn't when I was younger, but after the baby, a long litany of bodily changes—small emendations like this one—had bowled me over. Every time I talked to a friend or my mother, who lived in the Upper Peninsula, my observations were met with the same knowing, supportive tone. "I know," my mom would empathize. "Getting older sucks."

I reached for my phone, which was charging and face down on the nightstand, but not without a careful look at Cade first. His back was to me, the familiar landscape of black t-shirt over his skin. The sheet was down by his waist. Typical Cade. He was always hot. I was the one always snuggled up in fleece-lined sweatpants.

No messages.

I felt hollow.

And somehow, weirdly mad at Cade for talking me out of texting his mother at dinner.

"Just to check in," I'd said. "I don't need a call."

"Just let her be with her granddaughter," he'd said, a hint of annoyance in his tone.

I'd sighed and consented, putting my phone down, but now, I wish I'd thrown a question to Caroline, like a baited line in the water.

Then Caroline could have texted a picture of Ava. Or a cute selfie: Ava in Caroline's lap. As quietly as I could, I set the phone face back down on the smooth, modern nightstand. It looked like painted hardwood—pretty with brass pulls. We didn't dare have nice furniture. Gummy wasn't declawed.

Caroline was dependable—a retiree. Great health. She'd raised three boys, hadn't she? Nathan, Julian, then Cade. If anything were wrong with Ava, Caroline would know what to do.

Of course, Cade's dad had helped raising the three boys. He'd been such a kind man, too, and I was happy I at least got to meet him before he passed.

Cade was right. *I-know-better-but-I-won't-rub-it-in* Cade was right. Caroline was enjoying her time with Ava, the first girl in a handful of grandchildren. Nathan's wife had three boys, Julian's had had two; Ava was the family princess. No doubt they were doing fine.

I sighed, rolling over to my back. I let my hands travel to my belly, which still felt round and full from last night. Cade had suggested a place to try for brunch Sunday morning, but I wasn't sure how I was meant to eat again.

My fingers on my bare skin made me ache for Ava. I'd thought about her dozens of times since we left her at Caroline's house. I'd only asked Cade if he missed Ava twice. He'd said *of course,* his tone suggesting we ought to talk of other things.

I missed her. Ava. I missed her downy blonde hair—blonde! How? The c-shape curves of her cheeks. The way she balled her hands into fists. I missed the weight of her, the way she'd put one leg on each side of my torso and lean into me.

It was hard enough to be away from her all day, dropping her off at daycare so I could show up at the credit union on time. Customers calling to ask for current interest rates. Sometimes I wanted to tell them I didn't give a damn.

Recently, Ava had learned how to do raspberries, sticking her tongue between her pink lips. The sloppier the better. She'd learned from Cade who liked to dole out bad habits at bath time in the tiny tub he placed in the kitchen sink. Our apartment had no bathtub, just a small shower. I was dying for a house with a real tub, and as I rolled back over to my side trying to get comfortable, I told myself not to tell Cade we'd be $220 closer to a down payment if we'd just stayed the night in *our* bed. Not to mention seventy-five dollars, maybe more. He wouldn't let me see the bill the waiter brought in a black leather booklet. Maybe I could talk Cade into going home in the morning, remind him I make a mean omelet.

Before Ava, I did, anyway.

But I should just enjoy this, I thought, with a quiet sigh.

I wished again I could sleep like Cade. When Ava cried, he didn't hear her—at least not till she got loud. I heard her first, always, even when the baby monitor was eight inches from Cade's ear. I heard her first, raced to her crib first—often without Cade's knowledge. There'd already been a handful of mornings in our kitchen as Cade was filling his Stanley with coffee when he asked me if she woke in the night at all.

The unfairness of all that.

That mothers seem to carry extrasensory hearing. Maybe we became a little like wolves when we had our babies. I'd felt like a wolf more than a few times—a protective, howling mama wolf who would bare her white teeth at any threat, warn any predator away from her young.

Enjoy this, I thought, rolling over to my other side. *Stop being a wolf.*

I vowed right then that I wouldn't tell Cade how poorly I'd slept, how much time I'd spent laying there worrying about her. I didn't want to see the patience in his eyes wear thin if he knew our one special night away—our second anniversary celebration—I'd spent on anxiety.

As subtly as I could, I pushed up next to Cade, rested my forehead between his shoulder blades. He stirred a little, but he slept on. I closed my eyes and tried to match his steady breathing, praying for sleep to steal me away. I did the same thing at home after feeding and changing Ava. It was so difficult to fall back asleep after feeding her, changing her—after the adrenaline rush of hearing her cry over the baby monitor.

The baby monitor was an item I'd forgotten to add to the baby registry, so in the haze of the second day at home, I'd gone to Target in a messy rush and grabbed the cheapest set they had. As soon as the monitors were out of the box, I regretted my haste. I should have sprung for a better set—the top-rated ones. But no, I had to grab the cheapest box and jet out of there like a thief. They made monitors with video. I could have had a set that let me watch her sleep all night if I wanted to. Like an owl.

Although, owls didn't watch their babies sleep at *night*, did they? Owls are nocturnal. But maybe their young babies sleep at night?

This is the kind of thing Zach Blanchard would have made fun of me for, I thought, pressing my forehead deeper into the warm cotton of Cade's shirt. For not knowing. Or for asking, maybe. For wondering.

Zach thought I was weird. A strange girl. He'd told me as much as we were breaking up. We'd only dated three months, but what he'd said had stuck with me. Made me even more grateful Cade showed up so soon after the Zach disaster. Zach had said I was nice, and I was pretty, but I was a little too outside the box for him. Those were the words he'd used. I'd be perfect for someone else someday. But I wasn't right for him.

I was too outside of the box. Outside the box. Out of a box. Maybe I wasn't normal.

A normal person could sleep through the night—the *one* night she knew she'd be able to.

I sighed. Cade would be so disappointed.

You deserve it, he'd told me, over the top of his laptop the afternoon we'd made this overnight arrangement with Caroline. Cade had paid an extra twenty for a street-view room.

I willed sleep again, trying to ignore what I was sure were the first rays of dawn coming in through the thick-slat blinds of the large window. We'd forgotten to draw the blackout curtain. We'd talked about doing it, but then we'd let that slip. I was just wondering if I could ease out of bed quietly enough not to disturb Cade—I wanted him to sleep in—and then maybe I could fall back asleep and sleep in, too. Right then, from my side of the bed—on the fancy, mid-century modern, perfectly unscratched night-stand—came the unmistakable sound of the chorus of "Sweet Caroline."

BACHELORETTE PARTY

Miriam and Jamie

Miriam claims she's annoyed, but when the server asks if we'd care for anything else, round two gets ordered before I have the chance to say *we're fine.*

Our server, Jade, smiles and says she'll be right back.

I smile too, although I'm worried the red wine will wake me up in the middle of the night, as it sometimes does. Tonight, I want to get a good night's sleep.

"Are you doing a cake at least?" Miriam asks. Her eyebrows are up. She looks a little mad at me and perhaps she should be. I've sprung this on her, I know. But I also think she must have seen it coming.

"I don't think so," I say. "We're going to Bella Vita's. I'm sure they have a dessert menu."

"You're hanging the success of your second marriage on a *hope* that there's a dessert menu?"

I laugh, take a sip of the Merlot. In truth, I'd rather have ordered a beer, but I don't want to risk feeling bloated tomor-row in the dress I grabbed at Nordstrom Rack a week ago—a lovely ivory lace dress with short sleeves and a hemline that falls right above the knee. Miriam told me it needed alter-ations—to be taken in at the waist—but there is not time

130

for that. Besides, I'd told Miriam, Stan isn't marrying me for my waistline.

"You *are* coming to the dinner, right—you and Paul?"

Miriam nods. "Of course. Wouldn't miss it. You only get married twice once."

"Har har," I say. Jade returns with two glasses of wine, and I whisper to her that we're ready for the check whenever she gets a chance.

Miriam scoffs. "Come *on*. This is your bachelorette party!"

I shake my head. I can't drink the way I used to—*we* can't drink the way we used to. But something about being around Miriam makes me want to try.

When I look at her sometimes, I want to tell her she's like my diary come alive—the one person who knows all my secrets, everything I've been through. It's a privilege and a catastrophe to have someone walking around on the surface of Earth who knows my worst mistakes, my darkest features. But we call it friendship and keep doing it decade after decade.

To everyone else drinking and eating on the patio of the downtown bar Miriam picked for this Thursday in August, we look like two moms enjoying our wine.

"You remember your first bachelorette party?" she asks, grinning. "Remember that *guy*?"

"The guy who hit on you?" I tease. "Tall Guy?"

"Yeah. What was his name?"

"I have no idea," I say.

"I remember he gave me his email address!" Miriam giggles. "God. That was smooth."

"I think his name was Kurt," I say.

"Or Burt."

"Maybe it was Dirt," I joke.

Miriam snort-laughs as she sets down her wine.

"Your bachelorette party was way better," I say.

"Oh God," Miriam says. "Mine—I barely remember anything about mine."

"I know," I say. I smile conspiratorially at her. I am her walking diary, too.

Miriam sits up a little. "Don't change the subject. So, it's me and Paul. Who else?"

"Ethan and Eliza are coming," I say first. "Julianna, of course. Trevor and Amy—their kids, and Stan's."

"Ethan and Eliza—they're getting serious, huh?"

"Maybe," I muse. "They have been dating a few months. You never know."

I say this to Miriam knowing she is the queen of *you never know*. Her own husband, Paul—they were off and on for two years until they eloped one spring. It was for that reason I thought Miriam would understand a short engagement from me and Stan.

Stan and I were in our mid-fifties. Both of us had been married before; both of us had kids. We'd already been living together for a year. There was no desire for a big, fussy wedding. I called the courthouse, and they had a few slots available that Friday afternoon, and so why not? We didn't want a wedding party; we didn't want anything fancy.

We were just ready to be married.

That was what I thought Miriam would understand. And perhaps she did. Perhaps the real injury—not the fact that I didn't consult her on the dress I selected or the simple set of matching gold bands I'd picked up that week from the jeweler—was that I had waited a full day before telling her Stan and I were getting married, and to ask if she could come to the courthouse and then to a dinner afterward.

There had been no specific reason, no intention to keep Miriam out of the loop; rather, I'd sincerely been so busy, it had taken me time to call her. My first call had been to Ethan to make sure he could come, my subsequent calls to my brother and his wife, and then Stan's kids, and then to a few restaurants to see who could guarantee a reservation for a party of our size at seven p.m.

"So," Miriam says, picking up her second glass. "What about a photographer? A *videographer*?"

"I'm sure we'll take pictures," I shrug. "Someone will."

"*Someone* will," Miriam parrots. "You're just assuming the universe will offer you a perfect picture of your wedding to Stan—just like you're *assuming* there will be amazing dessert waiting for you."

Her disdain is funny, but I admit to myself I'm beginning to tire. I am thinking about the back-to-back appointments in the morning to get my nails and hair done. How I'd like to take a long bath, too.

"It's going to be fine," I say, smiling. "How's your wine?"

"Better than the first one," she says. "Just like your husband."

I grin at her dig at my ex. Then I ask, "Are you *actually* mad at me?"

She sets down her glass. She's thinking. A few feet away from us, a waitress sets down a big platter of empty glasses and I watch as they almost get toppled over when a man bumps into her. She makes the save at the last second.

"I just—are you sure this is what you want? I mean, what's the rush? The courthouse? Downtown? Are you pregnant?"

This makes me laugh hard. Miriam was the one I'd given my copy of *The Silent Passage* to last year.

"You're telling me that you and Stan want to get married in the same building you *both* got divorced in? I mean to different people but—I don't know, isn't that some pretty messed up karma?"

I hadn't considered that. I roll my eyes and sigh. "Don't be annoyed," I say gently. "I'm *really* happy. I can't wait to be married to Stan."

"You know I love Stan," Miriam says. "That's not the issue. Obviously, he's a big upgrade from what's-his-name."

I laugh again, despite myself. He was my husband for a decade, the father of my only son. The first and only of so many things. "I think you know his name."

"Michael," she quips. He was Mike, of course, but after he and I split up, Miriam only referred to him as *Michael*.

I supposed there were worse names she could have coined for him. Over the years, she had some less-than-flattering nicknames for a lot of the men I had dated. Her exes, too.

"Well, are you planning on being mad at me tomorrow?"

"Do you even have *flowers*?" Miriam asks.

I shake my head. "That's a good idea, though. I should swing by the grocery store and pick up a bouquet in the morning."

"*Oh my God*," Miriam moans—so loudly the couple sharing a charcuterie platter at the table next to us looks over for a moment. "You're gonna swing by Costco when they open at ten? Might as well pick up some toilet paper while you're there!"

To tease her, I act like I'm making a mental note of her suggestion. "We *are* kind of low on TP."

By now, Miriam's face is in her hands, and I'm studying the top of her head. For the past few years, I've seen gray in her roots where she gets lazy about coloring.

"No offense, Jamie," she says, "but you're really bad at getting married."

I laugh and take another gulp of wine. I picture Stan, sitting at home on our couch, probably having a beer, maybe putting away the dishes from our dinner. Half of me wishes I were home with him, watching something—a true-crime drama, like we like to watch, or something on HBO. "I did a really good job getting married the first time—remember?"

She nods. "Oh God, remember when Rich threw a bottle of beer?"

I laugh and shake my head again. "I still don't know how that was an accident."

She shrugs again and pushes her sunglasses on the table a few inches toward me. "He was dancing. You know how Rich loved to dance."

"I do," I say. For all the nicknames Miriam has given to her exes and mine, Rich Hooper was the one former boyfriend to whom she never gave a mean moniker. He was too much like her diary, too.

"At least the bottle was empty," I add.

"Anyway," she says, sighing. "I'm not trying to be a dick. I'm just—I just want to make sure this is what you really want." She looks at me. "I want you to have a really nice wedding."

I smile. "You'll be there with Paul. Ethan will be there. Stan will be there. His boys are coming. Trevor and Amy and their kids. Julianna. That's everyone. Not my mom; the trip would be too much for her right now, but she's happy for us. We'll go visit her next month."

Miriam's considering, and Jade is coming back with our bill. I pull out my credit card while wondering if I've done enough to convince her, but she's snatched the black book before I can and shoots me her best *how dare you* look.

"I just don't want you to look back and wish you had done a nicer wedding." Miriam's voice is gentler now as she puts her Visa into the black book's slot.

"I won't," I tell her. "I promise I won't. What I want—more than a nicer wedding—is a nicer *husband*."

She smiles. "That's the most you've trash-talked *Michael* in a while."

I shrug. "What can I say? He and I are better these days, now that Ethan's out of the house. Things are easier, the more time passes. You know how it goes."

She nods. "What does *Michael* have to say about your shotgun wedding?"

I smile, finish my wine. "He says, *Congratulations.*"

Miriam acts like she's thinking but I know she isn't. "That's nice of him."

"So did you ever email him?" I ask.

She's confused for a second, and I delight a little in still being able to pick up any old memory at any time, like it's a record I can put on, lower the stylus. Play any melody I want.

"I think I did," Miriam says. She stands up now, using the arms of her chair and smoothing out her skirt as she does. I follow suit, although my knees speak up in protest, a little stiff from sitting so long. "I don't remember what I said though."

"He ever write you back?" I ask. "Dirt?"

She chuckles. "Who remembers?"

We start walking to the patio's swinging half-door, Miriam giving Jade a wink and wave as we pass her.

"Thanks for the drinks," I say. "You know, this is the best bachelorette party anyone has ever thrown me."

Miriam laughs lightly as she adjusts her purse strap on her shoulder. "I can do better. For your next one, let's go to a *rave*."

I laugh out loud. "Deal."

We're about to part at our cars, and I look at her for another second. It's my habit when we're saying goodbye to make sure I have nothing else I want to tell her. I can't think of anything, though, and I know I'll see her tomorrow. In twenty-four hours, I'll be married to Stan and Miriam and I will be sharing champagne and some kind of dessert, laughing with our husbands and our kids. I'm so happy, I feel tears sting my eyes.

"You know," she says as she takes her keys out of her purse. "I think he *did* write me back. Eventually. Tall Guy. Dirt guy. But I really couldn't tell you what he said."

WHISPER MOMENT

We've been on the phone for forty-one minutes. My cheek is hot from my cell. Repositioning the phone to my other ear, I stand. Pilot stands, too.

I've changed my energy. I owe him a walk.

"How is that *not* a sign?" Chloe asks.

I picture her frowning, worry scrunching her face. I picture her hair pulled up in a ponytail, a headband smoothing the strays.

"I don't know."

Chloe sighs. I think she's dropped something in the sink. The water turns on.

"There's just—like I believe in *signs*, you know? *Whisper moments*—that's what Oprah calls it. Moments when your gut is telling you something. And you *can't* tell me it's a coincidence that the topic of her pod today was *signs your partner is cheating*."

I say nothing, just shift the phone back to my other ear. I've had to use the bathroom for twenty minutes, but Chloe is so worked up I haven't wanted to risk being on mute at a pivotal moment in the conversation.

"I'm sorry, Chloe," I say. "I'm worried I'm no help."

"I just—I don't know what to do. I'm *freaking out*."

I feel a sigh, but hold it in.

"Will you come over?" Chloe asks suddenly.

"*Now?*"

She might have asked me over an hour ago. Now, I'm in yoga pants—the pair I wear so often they never see the inside of my dresser. It's Tuesday. I've already planned the evening in my head: leftover lasagna, another glass of wine (or two), reality dating shows, a hot shower before bed.

Give all that up?

"Yes," Chloe says. "Maybe we can look."

"*Look?*"

"Yes," she repeats. "Please come over. I have wine."

I hesitate. Chloe's call has disrupted the routine, and no one is more aware of that than Pilot, who likes his walk before dinner.

"*Please?*"

"Okay," I say. "For a bit. I have an early day tomorrow—meeting first thing with the management team. I can't stay too late—or drink too much."

"Oh, thank you. Thank God. Yes, come over."

"Two things," I say. "One, I'm bringing Pilot, and two, you have to tell me what we're looking for."

"*Proof.*"

PILOT'S TAIL IS A SPIRITED metronome as I return from the bathroom and take his leash off the peg. I throw on my navy duster and shove my cell and keys into its generous pockets. My place is only four blocks from the rental she and Jake have shared for the past six months, and Pilot and I begin to walk toward it.

In my head, Chloe still lives across town, as she did when I met her. We'd worked for the same software consultancy for a few years—me as a designer, Chloe as a social media manager—until she landed a position at a bigger firm for more money.

"Come on," I say, urging him away from a tree. Pilot's head comes up just above my knee. I figure he's mostly hound—a tricolor with brown speckles on his white legs. He glues his nose to the sidewalk when we walk. However, he also has a penchant for sneaking food from the table; there must be some beagle lurking in his genes, too.

The animal shelter had described him as an "independent boy." Pilot had not disappointed.

As we make our way to Chloe's, a slight breeze blows at my sweater. The last hour of sunlight warms my face. Chloe's distress aside, it's a perfect October evening.

I try to remember when this started—the suspicion that Jake was cheating.

Chloe opened up to me one night when we'd gone out for drinks with some friends—my current co-workers, her former. I'd been ready to call it a night when she'd put her hand on my arm and asked if I had time for one more. Then, the conversation became long strings of *I know this sounds crazy, I just have a feeling, you're such a good listener.*

Jake often worked late on Friday nights. Or he sometimes came home an hour late. He'd claim he hit the gym, showered already, but Chloe would find his gym bag hanging on a hook in the laundry room.

Chloe said things like, "And I don't want to confront him, *you know*, because what if he's like, *hey crazy, I have an extra gym bag*. And what if he does?! And I'm just crazy?"

I became a confidante that night, and after, Chloe texted me things that happened.

She noticed he was always locking his phone. He got defensive one night when she used his laptop—only because she had left hers at the office and had wanted to write an email without laboring over her cell.

Pilot, oblivious, catches sight right then of a squirrel running up a tree a few feet away. The yank he gives nearly pulls my arm out of its socket. He runs to the tree, puts his two front paws on its thick bark, and bays. The squirrel is angry, chattering at us from a low branch.

"There," I say to Pilot, "you treed him. Happy now?"

"SO, WHAT ARE WE looking for, Nancy Drew?" I ask as Chloe opens the door. She's wearing leggings and an oversized sweatshirt, and from the look on her face, she's been crying. I soften.

"First, wine," she says. I apologize in advance for Pilot. I take off his leash. He looks at me, mildly confused, then wags his tail and heads to the kitchen.

"If you have any food on your floor, he'll find it," I joke.

Chloe follows and pours me a glass of red, then refills her own. The bottle is nothing special—a dark bottle with a burgundy top, adorned with a beige label. A Cabernet Sauvignon. The first sip bowls me over in my chair. It's wonderful.

"I'm sure I'm being stupid," she says. "I just—I can't shake this."

I take another big sip of wine, catching the taste of berries on my tongue. I do regret not grabbing something to eat before I left my place. I'm starving.

"Where's Jake now?"

"He's visiting his mom and staying the night."

"Where does she live?"

"Like an hour away—west of Lansing. He said he'd text me."

"Why is he staying with his mom?" I can't think of anything I know about Jake's mom, if she's ever come up before.

Chloe nods, takes another sip of wine. "Oh God—I can't believe I didn't tell you. His mom called him today and said someone had broken into her house."

My eyebrows raise. "Whoa. What? That sounds scary. Was she home when it happened?"

Chloe shakes her head. "No, she was at work. And she said she can't find anything missing. But she was *freaked* out, you know? She lives alone. Her stuff was *rearranged*."

I nod. Of course I know how scary it is to live alone. I've been on my own for a long time, although Pilot helps.

"Oh," Chloe says, "I didn't mean—"

I shake my head. "I'm not offended, Chloe. I'm in between relationships." I grin at her. "I just don't know what you're hoping to find," I add gently. "What kind of smoking gun? I mean, if he *is* cheating, what are we going to uncover?" I look around her kitchen for theatrical effect. "Are we shaking down his sock drawer? Reading his diary?"

She shakes her head. I realize she's considering. "I can't find a diary."

I pause. "Do you go through his things often?"

She shakes her head again. "I mean—*honestly*? On nights like tonight, I do. That's why I called you. I feel like I'm crawling out of my skin."

Pilot has finished his search of the perimeter and, apparently satisfied, sits at my feet. He's pouting because he wanted a longer walk than he got.

"Do you think he made up that story about his mom?" I ask.

Chloe looks like she's about to cry again. "I don't know. I just *feel* something."

"Well," I say after a moment. "Can you talk to him? About how you're feeling?"

She shakes her head. "What if I'm wrong? I'll *lose* him."

I take a deep breath and another sip of the wine. It's really good. I take a mental picture of the label and wonder how expensive it is. Probably, it costs more than I pay for wine, but I would splurge for this. My guess is Jake bought this one.

Jake works in finance at a bank—I know that much. He's also really attractive—I know that from Chloe's Instagram. He has dark hair and brown eyes, olive skin. Tall, athletic. Bright smile.

I don't say what I'm thinking: if your relationship is so fragile you can't talk about what's bothering you, the relationship is in trouble regardless of infidelity.

I don't say that. Who wants advice from a woman who hasn't had a relationship in years? Chloe must think I'm some kind of spinster, that I spend too much time alone. Every time I go out with her, she compliments my clothes, but tells me I would look better in something more revealing. She tells me I play down my cheekbones, my long eyelashes. She tells me I should take more chances, ask a guy out some time.

I do tell her, "You shouldn't feel this way in a relationship. You shouldn't *have* to feel this way."

"I know," Chloe says. She closes her eyes, but a second later, jumps when her phone vibrates on the counter. She grabs it. "Ugh," she says. "Just my mom."

She sets her cell back down. "I wish he'd text me."

"Hey," I say suddenly. "I have an idea."

"What?"

"Walk with me—with Pilot. Exercise clears your head. Have you had any today?"

She shakes her head, her ponytail swinging. "No. I've just had wine."

"It'll take your mind off Jake. I'm sure everything is fine. Maybe he's just giving all his attention to his mom. Sounds like maybe she needs it."

I'm not actually sure that everything is fine, but the longer I sit in her kitchen, hungry and restless, a little worn out from the day, the less I'll be able to help her.

If we're not going through his pockets for receipts or checking the collars of his white dress shirts for lipstick stains, I'm not sure what Chloe thinks we can accomplish. I start to realize maybe she just didn't feel like being alone.

I know that feeling well.

Chloe finishes her glass. "You're right. Let's walk."

Pilot raises his head at the word *walk* and comes over to Chloe, sniffing her hands as she stands up. "Well," I laugh. "You're pot-committed now."

Chloe asks if she can hold Pilot's leash, since the only dog she gets to walk is her parents' cocker spaniel, and she doesn't visit them often. We talk about work. She likes her new company, but she's struggling to communicate about projects with her supervisor and gets along better with her supervisor's supervisor. I catch her up on the latest news, too, but I'm not much for gossip—which Chloe knows. She's just being polite, or trying her best to follow my suggestion to push Jake out of her mind.

"Have you ever been in this kind of situation?" Chloe asks me, and I realize we're no longer talking about the juice cleanse she wants to try.

I shake my head. "I don't think so."

"You're lucky," she says. "It's the worst feeling."

I say nothing, just gesture we should turn at the next block.

"I just wish I could get a *sign*," Chloe moans.

"I thought you said Oprah was your sign," I tease.

She laughs. "Oh yeah. I forgot that. I mean, like—okay, that means *something*, but I want a *sign* sign."

"What would that look like?" I ask. "Are you waiting for *him* to say something?" Chloe looks horrified. Immediately, I regret it and start to open my mouth to apologize for my bluntness, to blame it on the wine, on being hungry.

"He'd—I mean, he'd only do that if he were breaking up with me, right?"

I start to answer when Pilot's leash whips out of her hands. He takes off at a full sprint.

"Oh my God!" Chloe yells, her hands flying up to her face.

"Pilot!" I yell.

But I know it's no use. Once a hound sees something he wants to chase, it's over. He's gotten loose before—twice— and both times were terrifying.

"I'm so sorry," Chloe says.

I tell myself not to panic. We'll find him. And above all, I tell myself not to make her feel worse.

However, I am wearing Tom's—no socks—and I do not feel like running, particularly after the wine.

I suck in a breath and start off anyway.

I hear Chloe running behind me, to my right. Pilot is a good fifty yards ahead of us—half a football field away. I think I see a rabbit, a flash of its white tail. I tell myself this won't be like the last time, the time my heart swam in my stomach with worry.

There is no feeling worse than worrying I'll never see him again—the fifty-five-pound hound who shares my queen-size bed.

I'm screaming the dog's name again. My duster is annoying to run in, all the extra fabric catching around my knees and calves. "*Pilot!*"

He can't hear me—or he won't. He's on the hunt, and everything in his body is telling him to pursue. Why did his instincts have to be so strong? The gap between us widens. I ask my legs to move faster, and the adrenaline gives me a burst as I run by a man on the sidewalk walking a corgi. He moves aside, realizing what's wrong.

I yell again, as loud as I can. I'm not sure if Chloe is close behind me or not. I feel my heart beating hard in my chest when I hear a noise that makes it sink to my feet: the definitive sound of tires screeching, and the dull clunk of a car crashing into something.

I'm not able to speak, just run. My heart is in my throat as I approach the black SUV. From what I can tell, it was turning right onto the road that Pilot was crossing.

Please, please, please, I beg inside.

A man gets out of the black SUV. He walks to the passenger side bumper, to where the damage occurred. He's crashed directly into a parked minivan, also black.

He crashed because he had to swerve.

He swerved to avoid hitting Pilot, whose tail is sticking out of a green hedge in front of the house on the corner. It's wagging—his tail.

Thank God.

Judging by that tail, he's got the rabbit cornered.

I read once that a beagle's tail is white at the end because it signals like a flag; it stands out in tall grass to alert a hunter. *Here's the duck you shot*, it says. *Right here!*

"Pilot!" I yell, partly to alert the man. I watch him glance at the house, perhaps wondering if the minivan's owner is coming out.

"Are you okay, sir?"

He nods his head.

Then my throat goes dry.

He doesn't recognize me.

Why would he? He's never met me.

"That's my dog," I say, a little apologetically as I walk toward the hedge.

As I approach Pilot, ready to grab the leash and hold it tighter than I ever have before, I look behind me to see if Chloe has recognized the driver.

With some effort, I pull Pilot from the hedge. He looks proud of himself. He has no idea how much he's scared me. I squat and rub his ears, stealing a glance at Chloe. She has her arms folded. Jake has his crossed, too, then his hands in his hair, then he pulls a phone from his pocket.

No one has emerged from the house we are standing in front of, and I'm thankful.

When Chloe starts walking toward us, leaving Jake at the curb, her face is a tight knot. Tears are on her cheeks.

"That *asshole*," she says. She can barely get the words out. I hug her, and she is shaking. I look over at Jake, who is behind the wheel of his SUV, slowly moving it in reverse. He does not look at us as he drives off.

No note for the minivan's owner, I think. No problem. Chloe can write down his number.

"I can't *believe* this."

I say, "It's gonna be okay."

By the jut of her chin on my shoulder, she's nodding.

She pulls away, wiping at her tears. Pilot is giving her his full attention, so she ruffles his ears and kisses him on the head. "I can't believe…"

I squat too, petting Pilot on the head. "I mean, you *did* say you wanted a sign," I offer.

Chloe laughs, then begins to cry again, so I say we should walk home. I know we'll talk about what Jake said—about what his excuses were, his lines. His lies. Where he had really been.

"Come on. We have an expensive bottle of wine to finish," I say, "although Pilot, we'll have to find some other reward for you."

IN TANDEM

He couldn't see Alcatraz from the base of the bridge, although he had looked for it twice.

Before their trip, Katie had watched two documentaries on Alcatraz. She had purchased a small travel guide of San Francisco, had soaked its pages with a yellow highlighter. She had bubbled over about the city's highlights. Her blue-green eyes had widened when she had talked about the infamous Alcatraz escapees.

"They were so brave," she had told him. "So determined."

"Or, they were idiots," he had snorted back.

Pat looked over again at Katie. She was standing a few feet from him. The whole trip, she'd been like a small moon constantly orbiting his larger body.

He liked it.

It was their first trip alone together. Katie had picked the perfect destination.

Although, it had taken a few hours for them to warm up to each other earlier in the week, to cut through the fog of strangeness that hung around suddenly spending twenty-four hours a day together. It was the first time they'd woken up together, brushed their teeth together. Pat had wiped out his savings account for the vacation, but he didn't regret it.

Because it had *all* been perfect, really. And to prove it to himself as he stood watching Katie rub sunscreen thickly onto her bare shoulders, Pat touched the front pocket of his jeans to feel the outline of the ring.

The ring had been nestled there since he had moved it from his duffel bag in an airport bathroom. He had felt too anxious to pack it with their checked luggage, but he was a nervous wreck anyway knowing it was in the overhead bin. During the flight, he kept staring at the compartment door, paranoid someone would steal his bag, or nervous Katie would look through the interior pocket when he was distracted and find the ring his mother had given to him—his grandmother's ring—squealing with delight as she pressed it into her palm.

In fact, the ring was starting to feel like a bit of an albatross.

Pat chuckled to himself. *I feel like Frodo—or maybe Samwise Gamgee*, he thought, having to admit to his round face and the extra pounds his midsection had carried since college.

It should feel reassuring, he thought, *the feel of the outline of the ring with its modest, antique solitaire diamond.*

Instead, a foreign thought flashed in his mind as Katie tucked the sunscreen tube into her bag and smiled at him: *I could chuck the ring into the Pacific Ocean.*

But he smiled back at Katie instead, pushing the thought out of his mind.

I'd be an idiot.

"Ready?" Katie asked.

"Ready. Let's cross."

EARLIER THAT MORNING, Pat and Katie had decided to rent bicycles to ride over the bridge—something Katie had set her heart on doing. When she saw that the rental shop offered tandems, she'd squeezed his hand until he'd acquiesced, despite the fact that he had never ridden one.

Pat was, however, the more experienced cyclist, so he faked an expert tutorial as they cautiously piloted the tandem away from the rental place. It was wobbly, and very challenging. Pat was sweating.

What he *wished* he had known—and probably should have guessed—was how difficult it would be to ride a tandem bicycle over inclines. Those famous San Francisco hills that had been setting his quads on fire all week—the ones that had made Katie beg for a piggyback ride on Lombard Street—were a deeper layer of hell on a bicycle built for two.

But they were in it now: somehow halfway across the bridge. The bike seemed to fight them with every pump of their legs. They were totally out of sync. He swore the gears were groaning. Pat tried to yell instructions, but quickly found Katie could barely hear him over the wind.

He felt like he was carrying both of them as they wove between the runners and the speed walkers. They were riding too slowly to keep up with the other cyclists, but too fast to ride safely with the pedestrians.

Suddenly it felt incredibly dangerous to be up so high in the middle of the Golden Gate, a stream of cars whirring by only yards away.

It was when Pat turned his head to yell again that he finally saw it: the small prison island isolated in the glimmering waters. He was staring at Alcatraz, trying to see any people, trying to see anyone in the water, for a few seconds too long.

"Oh my God!" Katie screamed.

They crashed into a side rail, the tandem folding into a heap like a flimsy house of cards. They were a jumble of limbs and wheels and steel. Katie burst immediately into tears, covering her head with her arms. She had two long scrapes on her left shin, Pat saw, and blood was already coming.

Pat tried to stand and realized he couldn't put any weight on his ankle. He bit his tongue to keep from crying. Somehow, he wrestled the bike away from her body.

Katie was sobbing.

I've ruined it, Pat thought. *Our perfect trip.*

He took off her rented helmet so he could wipe at her tears.

He knew he still had to try.

He wanted to make her face light up the way it had when she had first talked about the cable cars, the seals at Fisherman's Wharf, or about snuggling next to him on smooth white sheets in a nice hotel with the California sunshine streaming in.

He knew this was his impossible swim to shore.

Pat reached his hand—bloody knuckles and all—into the front pocket of his jeans, drew in a long breath, and held it.

CHRIST AT HEART'S DOOR

Miriam and Jamie

For a moment after my mother closed the bathroom door, I stood on the other side, listening. Water was rushing into the tub. I pictured my mother stepping out of her pink house slippers, her blue skirt, taking off her gold earrings and laying them by the soap dish.

After the faucet turned off, I walked the ten steps from the bathroom door to the desk by the exterior door that led to the garage. I wanted to call Miriam before eight.

I should be thankful to have a mother who could still bathe herself, I thought, sitting down at the desk and picking up the cordless phone from its cradle. Someday, she'd need help with that, too.

The mom who raised me could do anything. She was a whir of activity, always doing at least three things at the same time: making cookie dough and hard-boiled eggs while she waited for the yeast dough to rise; letting her hair set in curlers while she pulled on pantyhose. She couldn't watch television without knitting or darning socks or painting her toenails, a habit that spawned small red splotches on the carpet we all tried to ignore.

In her younger years, Mom probably would have started a bath, then paid some bills or pulled chicken breasts out of the freezer while the tub filled up.

Now, as an old woman, she only did one thing at a time.

"HI THERE," MIRIAM SAID. She'd picked up after the fourth ring. I wondered for a moment how she knew it was me since I'm not calling from my cell. Out in the middle of nowhere, Michigan, I barely sustained one bar.

"I have this number in as *Jamie's mom*," Miriam said.

"I don't remember ever calling you from this phone," I said.

I can almost picture her shrugging, just as I can picture her sitting on her couch with the remote on the cushion next to her, her cat, Schrödinger Five, in her lap.

"You must have, at some point. How are you?" Her voice sounded even, soft. In my head, the picture I had of her changes to one where she's holding a glass of red wine by its thin stem, a faint red kiss of lipstick on the rim.

Suddenly, I felt awash with exhaustion. I realized I was listening to my body for the first time in hours, and it's telling me it wants a glass of wine, too. I could get up and fetch one from the kitchen while I debriefed with Miriam, but I didn't want to. It weirdly felt like too much work.

Or maybe it was the paranoia that my elderly mother was like a young child now, and just as if she were a toddler, I should not stray more than those ten steps from the bathtub.

I picked at the phone's cradle, digging out trails of dust gathered in its crevices. Had there ever been a different phone on this desk? Not that my memory could recall. "This phone must be older than me."

"Are you calling me from a rotary?" Miriam teased.

"No. But it's old as dirt."

"How's your mom?" Miriam asked. "And don't think I didn't notice you dodged my first question, which was, how are you? You can answer in any order you see fit."

"I just wanted to give you a call before you settle in to watch your boyfriend," I said instead of answering.

Miriam's latest obsession was a new hospital drama that came on Tuesdays at eight and starred some actor she liked from a movie she dragged me to last summer. Even as I pictured his young, chiseled jaw on the big screen, the soft dimple in his left cheek that reminded me of my son when he was young, his name still escaped me.

"Oh, he can wait," Miriam said. "He's better on mute, honestly. Like most men," she added, though I know it was meant to make me laugh.

I sighed and, out of what I can imagine is a habit, looked up at the paper calendar my mom has on her wall. It was from nine years ago. It had been doodled and scribbled on from earlier use—phone numbers, doctors' appointments, a haircut, an oil change. Next to the calendar was a painting I had been staring at my whole life, one I knew so well, I felt sometimes maybe I had painted it, and just forgotten.

It was Jesus standing at the threshold of a wooden door, his hand prepared to knock. The painting—I looked it up once—was called "Christ at Heart's Door."

It appeared to be nighttime. Jesus was illuminated by some light source in the lower right-hand corner. It made his white robe glow. It made his skin bright, his hair shiny. The light made Jesus look vibrant and alive, although I wondered if I only thought that because I imagined all portrayals of Jesus as an adult were to remind us that he was about to die.

So young.

I wished my own son had lived to be thirty-three, but that wasn't in the cards for Ethan. And I couldn't attribute his death to a prophetic text or a Savior-like mission. Just to an impaired driver and bad fucking luck.

Jesus.

There he was, knocking at that door still. There was no knob or handle visible on the door—a metaphor, I'd read, that Christ would not force his way into your heart. You must be willing to let him in, to accept him.

He was standing there waiting, but I felt like I saw something different in the painting at that moment. His face had become more concerned. It seemed as if he wasn't not knocking anymore, but rather pointing.

Pointing at the front door.

As though saying, *open it, get in here.*

I felt like he was trying to tell me something—to go to the bathroom door, go check, go in.

We all find signs when we want to. *Where* we want to.

After Ethan died, I felt as though in small ways, the universe or God or Ethan himself was sending me little signs—moments. I had moments. I thought I would spot him in a crowd—but not *him*, exactly. Ethan through the ages. I would see a toddler who was perhaps two years old with brown curls, and I'd imagined it could be Ethan. Then, a month later, I'd see a seven or eight-year-old version of Ethan, but no. That wasn't him, either.

Once, a teenager who cut me off on the road looked so keenly like my son, I had to pull over at the next exit just to catch my breath.

It had even happened at the funeral. A handful of Ethan's friends from college had come. At least four times, I thought I saw Ethan standing among them. I hugged one boy in the funeral home longer than I should have, but he looked so much like Ethan, I wanted to feel his frame and confirm that he was athletic and slim in the same way my son was. I wanted to breathe in his hair and understand that he smelled like my son, like fresh laundry and Old Spice.

When the boy pulled away, I saw tears in his eyes. I wondered if I had embarrassed him, especially because I had been sobbing.

I wish I had asked his name. I wish he had offered it. I had no idea who that boy was. He probably understood my behavior as that of a grieving mother, not that my imagination had urged me to make him my son for my heart's own survival.

I was sorry I couldn't articulate it to him, but I wasn't sorry I'd held him the way I had. That boy had only come to the memorial service. He'd skipped the burial, the part where we committed Ethan's body to the ground.

I know that because I looked for his body more than any other in that crowd.

I PULLED MY EAR AWAY from the phone's receiver to decide if I could hear faint splashing, or if my mother was not moving at all in the tub. What if she'd drowned and I hadn't heard? What if her head slipped under the water and she couldn't pull herself up, and I'd been staring at Jesus and making jokes with my best friend on the phone like we were kids again, thinking about wine?

"Jamie?"

Miriam was in my ear. What a trick. She was so far away and somehow, right beside me.

"Sorry," I said. "Can you give me a sec? I'm going to check on Mom. She's in the tub."

"No worries," she said. "I'll be here."

I stood up and laid the phone on the desk, though I was aware I could have taken it with me. I was sure I was just being crazy, thinking that Christ at the door was trying to give me a sign.

OF COURSE, JESUS WAS WRONG—or rather, he was just asking to be let into that house in that painting, not telling me I am a negligent daughter.

I rapped my knuckles on the bathroom door.

"I'm almost out honey, do you need to use it?"

"No," I said. "Take your time."

I was about to walk back to the desk, back to Miriam, when I made a quick diversion to the kitchen. I grabbed a juice glass from the cupboard and filled it two-thirds of the way with the Merlot I'd brought.

I took a big sip as I sat back down, under the watchful eyes of Jesus.

"Sorry," I said again. "She's fine."

"Good," Miriam said. "Was your drive okay?"

"Yeah. Long, but, you know. Stan can't get away this week."

"Mmm," Miriam said. "You'll stay through Friday?"

I had told Stan I could handle this trip to check on Mom alone since she was released from the hospital for a blood pressure scare, no problem. But within an hour of arriving, I had instantly regretted sounding so sure of myself. All afternoon, I fought the urge to call him at his office and ask if he could move his calendar around.

"I think so." I took another sip of the wine. If I stayed all week, I'd need another bottle. That was fine. I should make her meals, stock her fridge anyway. I'd already chucked a ton of expired food that afternoon.

"You call me tomorrow?" Miriam said.

"I will." I took another sip of wine, smaller this time. It was hitting me harder than it should. I hadn't eaten much, I realized. I stopped for coffee on the drive, and there had been an apple at some point. I only picked at the pasta bake I had put together for our dinner. It tasted bad. Maybe those canned diced tomatoes had expired.

"How are you anyway? I'm sorry, I haven't even asked."

"Oh, I think I'm in *love*," Miriam said in a voice I happened to know she thinks is sexy. I'd heard it for so many years, and it still made me smile. "What's the rule on age difference again? Half your age plus seven? Or is it minus seven? Am I too old for this kid?"

I laughed, said yes, and looked up at Jesus again. As a Jewish woman, Miriam would find the prevalence of

Christian relics in this house particularly amusing. I considered telling Miriam about the painting—what I read about its meaning—but I'd already kept her on the phone longer than I meant to. And although she would never say it, I imagine she was ready to hang up and get back to her show, back to stroking Schrödinger Five on the couch.

We talked for another minute or two about her plans to have lunch with her daughter Julianna tomorrow, then to volunteer at the library. They were preparing for their bi-annual fundraiser. There was a doctor's appointment at the end of the week. She needed to be more consistent with the stretches prescribed to her by her physical therapist.

Finally, I let her go. I pictured her unmuting her show as I hung up on my end.

But before I rose from the desk, before I walked to the bathroom to help my mother out of the bathtub and into a towel, I raised my half-empty juice glass in a toast to "Christ at Heart's Door."

"Hey," I said. "Thanks anyway. You've been a big help." I downed my drink in one and walked the ten steps back to the bathroom, the daughter at the bathroom door.

ACKNOWLEDGMENTS

Thank you to the readers and editors of the various literary magazines and anthologies in which versions of these stories first appeared:

"Antique Desk" originally appeared in *Coffee Ring* magazine.

"Arrangements" originally appeared in *Product Magazine* (as "Split Level").

"Bachelorette Party" originally appeared in *Grand Dame Literary Magazine.*

"Christ at Heart's Door" originally appeared in *Vagabond City.*

"Cusping" originally appeared in *The Taborian.*

"Fifth Circle" originally appeared in the *2016 Write Michigan Anthology*; the story took first place in the Readers' Choice category of the annual state-wide short story competition.

"In Tandem," "Interwoven," and "Loggerhead" originally appeared in *Cardinal Sins;* "In Tandem" took first place in a flash fiction contest.

"The Only Private Place" originally appeared in *The Lakeshore Review*, Fall 2022. An excerpt originally appeared in *The Offbeat: Collection Glances—a literary collection* (2005).

"Psychic Reading" originally appeared in the community anthology, *The Drifter and Other Unusual Tales* (Pages Promotions, 2022).

"Restoring Notre-Dame" originally appeared in *Literaria Magazine*.

"Stag's" originally appeared in *The Candid Review.*

"Visitor's Pass" originally appeared in *Surface Reflections* (Lakeshore One, 2022).

"Whisper Moment" originally appeared in *Litbreak Magazine.*

* * *

When I was an undergraduate at Michigan State University, I was fortunate to have the opportunity to study fiction under Gordon Henry and creative non-fiction under Marcia Aldrich. During my senior year, I began drafting a piece for Dr. Henry's class that grew into "The Only Private Place." In 2005, I entered it in MSU's annual Jim Cash Creative Writing Awards. Reader, believe me when I tell you, it was the shock of a lifetime when it won.

That was twenty years ago!

And what's funny is that after I graduated, I more or less stopped writing. From age twenty-two to thirty, I wrote only a few poems and one short story. (It's so bad. It's not in this book. It aptly languishes, along with those bad poems, in Google Drive.)

I couldn't tell you what held me back for the better part of a decade, other than to say I didn't want to write. I wasn't ready, or I wasn't myself. I wasn't sure I had much to say. I wasn't unconvinced someone else should have won that award.

But slowly—and I mean at a turtle's pace—I came back to writing. I started crafting an essay the summer I turned thirty-one while participating in the Lake Michigan Writing Project. When I was pregnant with my daughter a year or so after that, I started jotting little lines of poetry here and there. I was grateful to learn that writing had no interest in holding my absence against me. It let me come back freely. Writing holds no grudge against its prodigal sons.

Many of the stories in this book were written when my children were babies. When I read those stories now, I remember the rush to write during naptime on the broken IKEA dresser my husband fashioned into something with utility. I wrote and I wrote, both waiting for the babies to wake up and hoping they would sleep on.

There's no one around to pull me off the stage with a hook, so let's have me go after a few more words of thanks:

Thank you Norman Belanger, Garrett Stack, and Megan Turner. I love our Snazzy group.

Thank you to my Spalding University MFA family.

Thank you Ellie Atkinson, Dr. Ross Tangedal, and the amazing team at Cornerstone Press (as noted on the copyright page). I'm really grateful for all of you—and Ellie, especially, who pushed all these stories to be better.

Thank you Bonnie Jo Campbell, RS Deeren, Nathan Gower, Caitlin Horrocks, and Phillip Sterling. There's no feeling quite like that of reading words of praise from writers one admires.

Thank you, Greg Pape, for lending me your quote.

Thank you Melissa Fox for swooping in to help me with these stories! I'm grateful for your sharp eyes and your support.

Thank you to my family—especially my parents and my sister. I'm so lucky to have always lived surrounded by your love and support. Thank you to my children, Mara and Lincoln.

And thank you, forever and always, Micah.

Colleen Alles is a writer, librarian, and Michigan girl for life. A graduate of Michigan State University and Wayne State University, she's currently pursuing her MFA in poetry from Spalding University. Colleen is also a contributing editor (short fiction) for *Barren Magazine*. This is her debut short story collection. When she isn't reading or writing, she's either playing with her kids or spoiling her beagle. You can find her at www.colleenalles.com.